Courting Disaster...

Ronnie had to get away, but the kayak business was at the end of the dock and there was nowhere to go except into the water. The water looked clean...

Who was she kidding? It was a good way to be noticed and it would leave Maddy unprotected. Trying to be casual, Ronnie spun around from Seth and his impending tour, crossed to Maddy, scooped her up and ducked them both into the equipment shed. It was a small building about fifteen feet by ten in one corner of the dock and crammed full of PFDs, paddles, hoses, and sundry kayaking equipment. She pressed into the shadows of the rear corner, next to a stack of old PFDs that stank of salt rot and old canvas. Now she was truly cornered. And if she refused to come out and help Seth with the tour, she might as well kiss her precious job goodbye before she'd ever had a chance to really get started.

"Mommy? What's going on?"

Ronnie held her finger to her lips, because even whispering, Maddy's clear voice carried. "Let's be really quiet and pretend like we don't want the people outside to hear us, 'kay?"

Maddy's open expression turned serious. "Is it—is it the bad man?"

Ronnie frowned. "The bad man?"

"The bad man that I dream about sometimes. He makes you cry."

Maddy's worried expression was enough to break Ronnie's heart. She pulled her baby into her chest. "No, baby, it's not the bad man. There'll be no bad man ever again, I promise." Not as long as she had breath in her lungs. "Now let's just stay quiet, okay?"

Maddy snuggled in and nodded just as a tall, male figure blocked the sun-filled doorway.

Fantasy and Romance by Karen L. Abrahamson

Romance
Second Spring
Judas Kiss
Coming Down Christmas
Shades of Moonlight
Shadow Play
Ashes and Light

Unlocking Her Heart
Unlocking Her History
Unlocking Her Grace
Unlocking Her Dreams
Unlocking Her Chances
Unlocking Her Doubts

Surviving Safe Harbor

Fantasy
The Warden of Power
Impossible
The Cartographer's Daughter
The American Geological Survey Series:
Afterburn
Aftershock
Aftermath
Afterimage

Terra Incognita
Terra Infirma
Terra Nueva

Other Fantasy Novels
Ice Dragon
Emberstone
Mutable Things
The Crystal Courtesan

SURVIVING SAFE HARBOR

KAREN L. ABRAHAMSON

SURVIVING SAFE HARBOR

Print edition published by Twisted Root Publishing January 2018.

Surviving Safe Harbor Copyright © 2018 by Karen L. Abrahamson.

All rights reserved, including the right of reproduction, in whole or in part in any form. This book is a work of fiction. Names, characters, places and incidents either are products of the author's imagination or are used fictitiously. Any resemblance to actual events or locales or persons, living or dead, is entirely coincidental.

ISBN: 978-1-927753-62-0

Cover design by Twisted Root Publishing

Cover images: © artfotoss|depositphotos.com, and photonatura|depositphotos.com

For more information about Twisted Root Publishing, please visit our website at http://www.twistedrootpublishing.com.

SURVIVING SAFE HARBOR

CHAPTER 1

Ronnie Baxter sat with her knees pulled up to her chest on a life jacket cabinet on the forward viewing deck of the massive ferry. The wind tangled in her long hair. The deck throbbed with the engines, but the vibrant air was filled with salt brine and gull cries—so different from the cloying landlocked life she'd lived for so long. It was almost like coming back to life again—if she could quit looking over her shoulder.

Her four-year-old daughter Maddy—short for Madeline—sat beside her in her favorite pink hoodie and leggings, holding up pieces of her sandwich for the gulls. It was a pretty sight. Maddy's hair, a shade blonder than Ronnie's strawberry blonde, streamed against the pink of her clothing. The green of the rugged B.C. coastal mountains and the blue of sea and sky served as backdrop.

Under the warmth of the sun, watching the joyous way that white-winged gulls slipped through the air, Ronnie almost believed that there was a future for the two of them. That they'd finally left behind all the darkness.

A gust of wind chilled Ronnie. Maddy let the last bit of her sandwich fall to the deck.

"It's cold, Mommy." She cuddled into Ronnie's side and a single gull showed bravado, swooped and scooped up the fallen bread only to be attacked by the other gulls for a piece of his bounty. They flew off screaming.

Ronnie inhaled Maddy's baby shampoo scent and shivered.

"Why are they doing that, Mommy? That one seagull was brave and got the bread all by himself?"

Ronnie hugged her daughter a little closer. "Some people think you should always share, sweetie."

At least, shared custody was what the judges and lawyers had said, regardless of all the proof of spousal abuse. They couldn't or wouldn't believe that there were already signs that the violence was spreading to Maddy, and that was a potentiality Ronnie couldn't allow to develop.

She kissed Maddy's soft hair. "Next time we'll have to remember to bring more bread. You remind me, 'kay?"

Maddy nodded.

The massive car ferry chugged around the string of islands that filled the entrance to Howe Sound. Ahead, by the water at the base of a mountain, was what looked like a tangled scaffolding. "Look. There's where we're going." She pointed.

"And where's our house going to be?"

Where indeed. Ronnie checked over her shoulder. "We have to find a house, sweetie. We're going to have an adventure and camp for a little while."

Until she could find daycare and a job that could pay for everything. After all the lawyer's bills from fighting her husband's demands, she didn't really have—in her dead father's words—the proverbial pot to pee in or the window to throw it out of. The world felt very lonely.

The ship's engines changed rhythm and Ronnie stood. "I think we better head down to the car."

Maddy jumped down beside her and headed for the rail, Ronnie hovering behind her. The high decks made her nervous—not that the decks didn't have plenty of rails, but four-year-olds had a knack for finding ways through boundaries. Just like Maddy had burst full-blown into Ronnie's heart the moment she'd realized she was pregnant. It might not have been a planned pregnancy—something that had infuriated Jared, something he'd demanded she end—but it was still the best thing that had ever happened to Ronnie. Even if it had marked the beginning of the end for her marriage.

No way was she letting her little girl be raised by a violent man.

"Look, Mommy! There's a man in the water!" Madeline's young voice carried and caught the attention of other passengers.

"Where, honey? Where?" Because a man in the ocean had about ten minutes to get himself out before the cold and the waves took him. She at least remembered that from her time as a kayak guide years ago. Before marriage had turned her timid.

Maddy was pressed up against the rail pointing down into the water.

Ronnie followed the length of the chubby little-girl arm and saw...

Waves. A light chop. No sign of a boat or kayak. A swimmer? But it was an awfully long way from shore and no swimmer in their right mind would swim right into the ferry's route.

A shadow passed under the waves as if there was something there. Then a head bobbed up in the water and looked up at her. Dark, intelligent eyes met hers. An aquiline nose and wide mouth and then something happened—a shimmer of light on water—and there was a gray, furred head and black nose.

Ronnie stumbled back from the rail. What had she just seen?

"It's just a seal," said a young man with a backpack who had joined them. "No person'd be stupid enough to swim out this far in the ocean."

Maddy frowned. "But it was a man. I saw a man." She looked confidently up at the backpacker.

"It couldn't have been a man, sweetie. Look." Ronnie pointed back at the waves as the seal rolled in the water exposing speckled gray-and-black hide before he dove. "That's a seal. People don't have spots like that."

Maddy shook her head. "I saw a man."

"Isn't that sweet. She's so sure. You are a sharp-eyed little one," cooed a grandmotherly type with the steel gray eyes of a jail guard. "She really is a sweet one," the woman said, looking at Ronnie.

Getting the once over from someone—a few someones, given Maddy's cry had brought a number of people to the rail—wasn't exactly the way to remain anonymous.

She couldn't afford to be memorable. Ronnie caught Maddy's hand and tugged her back from the rail. "She has a vivid imagination. Come on, sweetie."

She hauled Maddy after her, through the door into the ferry and out of the wind, then down the many stairs to the rumble and engine noise of the car decks. She keyed them into the ancient Civic hatchback and collapsed into her seat in the comforting scent of old fast food wrappers and yogurt tubes. Their lone suitcase sat in the hatch amid sleeping bags, toys, and Maddy's favorite teddy bear.

Ronnie's heart was pounding. So were her ears. She inhaled and closed her eyes. There was too good a chance that Jared would figure out what she'd done instead of going to Disneyworld as she'd announced. With her arrival back in Chicago long past due, Jared would be looking for them. So would the authorities. And with her dual citizenship, it wasn't hard to figure out that she might run back to her mother's home country. The fact that she had never been to the west coast was her one hope. Jared would figure she'd go to a place where people she knew could help her. But there was still the potential for her or Maddy's face to be publicized in the media. They couldn't afford to be memorable.

"Mommy? Are you all right?"

Ronnie opened her eyes and winked in the rearview mirror at her daughter in her child's seat.

"Never better," she said, mimicking the British accent of the actress in her daughter's favorite wizarding movie.

Maddy's grin wiped out the concern that had placed a little line between her eyes. "Never better, indeed."

It was a favorite game between them.

The ferry engines slowed and loudspeakers announced that it was time for passengers to return to their vehicles. Through the open windows on the car deck waited the forested folds of the mountains, the rocky shorelines, and the small towns of a place optimistically called the Sunshine Coast.

§

Three days later, and still tasting the remains of yet another lunchtime peanut butter sandwich, Ronnie sat on a towel at the beach at the Roberts Creek Campground and counted what remained of her cash one more time. Maddy played in the ocean fifteen feet away. A piddling three hundred Canadian dollars and change, and the campsite was costing her twenty dollars a night. She had to find a job—there was only so long they could survive on peanut butter and jelly—but so far her ventures into the Roberts Creek businesses and even into Sechelt, the larger town farther north, hadn't landed her a job that could pay for rent or even pay for her current bills. Heaven knew she needed to get herself and Maddy settled before school started if they were going to make a go of it here. The trouble was, living in a campground didn't exactly put you in touch with the locals who might know of a job, and all of the local restaurants, shops, and grocery stores seemed to have filled their quota of summer employees—or if they hadn't filled them, they were only interested in hiring locals.

She stuffed her wallet back in her shorts and hugged her tanned knees anxiously while Maddy explored the small tidal pools along the shore. The sky was a perfect blue with puffy white clouds. Her daughter was the perfect blonde-haired child with natural ringlets down her back that caught the wind, her favorite orange bathing suit a natural foil against the blue backdrop. The forest rolled down to the crescent of beach, scenting the briny air with cedar. A perfect paradise for those who could afford it—made more picturesque by the phalanx of brightly colored kayaks rounding the point of the cove. The kayakers at the front and rear of the group had the easy even strokes of experienced paddlers. The middle eight did not—too much splashing, too high an angle for the paddles or the paddles barely touching the water.

A tour, then. That was the usual formation she'd used with a group of inexperienced paddlers long ago when she'd still been single and before the rest of her life had happened. Watching the paddlers across the water, she felt the ghostly pull and release of the muscles across her shoulders and back and settled back on the towel, her legs out before her just as they'd been in a kayak. Funny how the body remembered.

The group of kayaks came into shore. The leader deftly leaped out of his boat and hauled it up the beach before rushing back to catch each of his charges as they came into shore. Tall and tanned, eyes and dark hair shielded beneath sunglasses and a ball cap, she couldn't say what his face looked like, but the rest of him was deserving of a second or even third look. Typical summer employee looking to buff up his tan and his flirting among the female tourists. The kayaking companies back home had been full of that type—seasonal drifters who spent the winters bumming on the ski hills.

But there was nothing the matter with looking, was there? Strong shoulders with the roped muscle of the athlete who carried very little extra fat. Developed biceps and triceps from all that paddling, and a tattoo she couldn't quite make out on his left arm. Long swimmer's legs and large hands and feet. She hauled her study away, too aware of the old saying of what went along with large hands and feet. It had been three months since she left Jared, and while looking didn't hurt, there was no way she was getting involved again.

When she looked up again, those aviator sunglasses were tipped in her direction and she felt herself color as if he'd heard what she'd been thinking. She was pretty sure the eyes behind the glasses were assessing her faded cutoffs and worn, sleeveless t-shirt and finding her wanting.

She leapt up and strode over to Maddy. "So what are you discovering?"

"There are little crabs and clam shells!" Maddy proudly held up her bounty, then looked past Ronnie. "So are those the kind of kayaks you used to have, Mommy?"

Ronnie turned beside her. "Well, yes. They sort of are. Except Mommy's kayak was the color of the sky."

"Pretty," Maddy said.

"It was." But then Ronnie realized Maddy wasn't talking about the blue kayak lost in the sea of time. She was eyeing the rainbow of kayaks now brought up into a neat line on shore, while the paddlers gathered not too far from Ronnie's towel and were sharing around bags of carrots, packages of hummus, slabs of pita bread, and packages of sandwiches. The scent of ham and mustard, and tuna and cheese wafted over the cove.

"It smells good," Maddy said, just a little too loud.

It did. Ronnie's mouth watered far more than it ever would again over peanut butter and jelly. "It does smell good, but we just had our lunch. Remember?"

Maddy sighed and looked up at Ronnie with too-weary eyes. "Mommy, I'm really tired of peanut butter and jelly. Can we have something else tonight? I really like tuna sandwiches."

"Hey! If you like tuna, you're welcome to one of mine. I have them all the time." The deep voice reminded Ronnie a little of waves hitting a rocky shoreline and the gentle spray that would mist up and cover your skin. She shivered.

Of course the speaker was none other than aviator sunglass boy. He stood up from his perch on a driftwood log and sauntered over, a neatly wax-paper-wrapped sandwich in his hand. "Here you go. If I do say so myself, it's a good tuna sandwich. A secret recipe—one of my specialties."

Maddy hesitated, awaiting Ronnie's approval. There was something about the guy. Something familiar, and yet he was about as different as possible from the guys Ronnie knew. By the squint lines edging out of the sunglasses, he was older than she'd first thought, too. Thirty-six or-seven—a few years older than her. It was weird the way a place low down in her belly tingled pleasantly just standing beside him. But she was staying low profile, remember?

"This really isn't necessary. I can make my daughter a tuna sandwich."

The proffered sandwich lowered a little, but the wide mouth stretched in a grin that revealed even, white, male-supermodel teeth. "I'm sure you can, but your daughter seemed to have a hankering right now and I happen to have an extra sandwich."

He shifted the sandwich into his other hand and held out his hand in greeting. "Seth Cullen."

Ronnie hesitated but then accepted his grip—firm, callused, so this wasn't just some pretty boy. "Ronnie Baxter. This is Maddy, my daughter."

"Well how do you do, Maddy? You know, you really could help me out by taking my sandwich. I always make too many of them and then I have to eat them myself. If I don't eat them, they go bad, you know." There was just the slightest of lilt in his voice that made Ronnie think of Gaelic songs, fishing boats, and fiddles, but then the accent faded as if he was tucking that part of him away. For all he was a tour leader and in the public eye every day, this man carried secrets with him.

She didn't trust secrets—not that she didn't have them herself.

But Maddy gravely accepted the crisply-wrapped sandwich. "Thank you. I'm sure I will enjoy it."

Lord, she sounded about fifty, not four, but living through a violent home life could age a child the same as the mother.

"That was politely said," Seth said.

"I've tried to raise her right." Ronnie leaned down to her daughter. "Why don't you go sit on our towel and eat your sandwich. That way you can tell Mr. Cullen how much you've enjoyed it."

Maddy scampered off and Ronnie looked up at Seth Cullen. He really was tall. And decidedly good looking even though she couldn't see his eyes behind his sunglasses. Better yet, he wasn't one of those guys who seemed to know it and revel in the fact that every woman around was noticing. He wore an old, sleeveless t-shirt, its red so faded it was almost pink. On the front, also faded, was an emblem of a coastline with the words Coastal Kayak encircling the coastline. Encircling his right bicep, the tattoo revealed itself to be a seal twined with either a piece of translucent green seaweed or a scarf. It was amazing the way the artist had caught the light in the fabric.

"I take it you're a tour leader," Ronnie said, to break the uncomfortable silence.

"Yup. Something to do every summer. I bring groups out on day and overnight trips."

"Nice boats. All fiberglass. Usually companies just use plastic for their hires."

He nodded. "Plastic's sturdier and takes more abuse, but they don't have as much resale value."

"I remember. But these are either new or you've kept them in darn good condition."

He shrugged. "This is their second year, but I'm pretty careful what beaches we come to. And I threaten the rentals with physical harm if they hurt the boats." He leaned in and stage whispered the latter and then chuckled. "You seem to know about kayaks."

Ronnie shrugged. "It was a long time ago, in another life. I led tours myself. It was on the east coast. I haven't been in a kayak since, but I still remember it fondly." More than fondly, actually. She'd once tried to get Jared out in a kayak because Chicago wasn't exactly without access to shoreline, but it 'hadn't been his thing' and so she'd been told in no uncertain terms that she was expected to not have it be her thing either. That was when they were engaged, when Jared was still weaning her away from her friends. Before things turned bad.

She shivered and came to herself standing on a patch of sand in the west coast sunshine that had suddenly faded to cool. Seth Cullen looked down at her. Even at five-foot-seven beside him she felt small and she stumbled back a step. She wasn't going to let herself feel vulnerable anymore.

"Just where were you?" he asked, catching her elbow to steady her. His touch set a warm tingle right down to her core, and even with his eyes hidden, his expression was concerned.

She shook her head and tugged loose. "Nowhere that matters. Thinking about kayaks."

His mouth downturned. "It didn't look anyplace good. What, a kayak bite you sometime?"

She laughed and the dark memories passed. "No bites. One or two dunkings way back at the beginning. Nope. Kayaks were only a good thing."

His expression then turned calculating and he stepped in close and lowered his voice. "Listen. I've got to get this crew moving because they clearly are going to struggle going home against the current, but if you ever want to go out, why don't you give me a call. And if you're here for a while and interested in making a couple of dollars, maybe you'd be interested in helping out with the boats. We don't pay a lot, but it gets you out in the sunshine." He dug in a pocket of his baggy shorts and fished out a laminated business card with a non-faded version of the logo on his t-shirt.

She hesitated, but took it even though she knew she'd never use it. Seth Cullen, aka aviator shade guy, was a mite too attractive and she had no room in her life for that.

After thanking him for the card and the sandwich, she retreated to Maddy, who was busily vacuuming the sandwich down, all but the crusts—as usual.

"You know that all the best stuff is in the crusts, right?" she said as she settled beside her daughter.

"Never better, I know, but I thought that you like them so much, I'd save them for you, Mommy." Such an angelic face, before she broke into a gap-toothed grin.

"Never better, sly girl," Ronnie said and pulled Maddy into her side for a tickle before filching one of the crusts to chew on. It was—wonderful. The sweet-salt taste of tuna and relish and mayo tanging the bread was even better than she remembered. And totally beyond the budget of a woman trying to stretch a finite few dollars into an infinite future.

Seth Cullen and his assistant guide were busy settling their charges into their kayaks and shoving them back into the emerald-green cove. When the group was loaded, Seth shoved his boat into the waves and lightly slipped aboard as if he was made for the water. He raised a hand in her direction and then used his paddle to dragonfly across the water to lead his hesitant charges back around the headland. She liked the way his back muscles worked smoothly under his skin, almost as if man and kayak were one and the same.

Ronnie looked down at the business card and chewed another crust of tuna-infused bread. Seth Cullen was an attractive guy—not her type, because she was more into blonds—but there was something about him. Something that set a tingle in her skin that left her sorely tempted to call him. Thank God the last few years had taught her never to trust her feelings. 'If she ever wanted to go out,' indeed!

She flicked the card between her fingers. Seth Cullen. Had he actually been offering the chance for a job, or had he just been flirting?

CHAPTER 2

The early morning sun played over the back of Keats Island and filled Gibsons Harbor with golden light as Seth gave his fleet of fifteen kayaks another once-over. Tour boats, sailboats, and pleasure craft chugged out the channel past the breakwater toward the blue water and winds of Georgia Strait or the more sheltered waters of Howe Sound. Voices, music, and the sounds of crockery came from the restaurants that overlooked the harbor. Summer people lugged their suitcases and coolers on rumbling wheels down the wooden wharf, headed for the water taxis that would take them out to their summer homes on the islands off shore. Hopefully, up in the Coast Kayak shop, Carol Dermott was taking reservations for more tours. The weather was prime for it. The season was, too. The delectable scents of scrambled eggs, bacon, and coffee wafted out from the restaurants and the few permanent residences of the harbor.

Seth's stomach rumbled. The quick coffee and bowl of organic muesli was wearing off already, darn it. Usually he made himself a good solid breakfast of porridge or an omelet, but he'd missed out these past two days because he'd slept through his alarm. He hadn't slept well both nights, having lain awake thinking of a brief encounter in Roberts Creek. Ronnie Baxter had made an indelible impression in their brief meeting—more so than the fleeting first glance he'd had of her on the ferry. The cloud of red-blonde hair that seemed to net the breeze; the fair skin, tanned golden. She'd been tall for a woman, and slim as a sylph, but it was the wariness of her gaze that haunted him. Ronnie Baxter was a woman who feared life. He'd found his brain churning over and over, wondering what she was afraid of and what made her afraid of him.

But enough about a woman he would likely never see again. He couldn't afford the problems it would bring.

He focused on the kayak in front of him, a brilliant red Venture made locally to specifications that he had provided. If you were going to be safe on the water, the boats had to be stable and they needed to be regularly inspected. If you wanted to be a popular tour company written up in the guide books, you needed to make sure your boats were pristine and well-functioning. Even a sticky footrest adjustment cord could draw complaints and lower your five-star rating.

Seth practically turned himself upside down, trying to see what was jamming the footrest in the Venture kayak. It was a great boat, but at two years old, it was nearing the end of its working life. He'd put it out to pasture and sell it at the end of the season.

He reached in and—darn it, something was in there, holding closed the little mechanism that allowed the footrests to slip along the cord that guided the kayak's rudder. The good thing about kayaks was that they were pretty simple boats. The problem with kayaks was getting at the few places that could have problems. His head and shoulders were too broad to get into the cockpit and, unable to see while he worked, it was hard to figure out how to remove whatever was jamming the darn thing. What was going on? Usually he could fix these silly things with a flick of his fingers. But this morning the high tide that usually filled him with a comfortable sense of purpose and accomplishment wasn't working.

He leaned over to get a better picture of what he was up against, but the shadows in the depth of the cockpit hid the culprit.

When he brought his head up, he was gifted with the view of a set of long, tanned legs that he was pretty sure he recognized. The glare of sun was behind the owner of the legs, but the legs themselves were worthy of attention—long, lean, and muscled like a runner or swimmer. He happened to like both kinds of legs. He blinked and shaded his eyes, but it didn't help any more than his shades or his baseball cap visor.

"May I help you?"

"Maybe I can help you. You've been fussing over that boat for a while." Feminine voice. Cool and business-like and two days ago when they'd met the voice and legs went with a cloud of red-gold hair, clear blue eyes, and an upturned nose. His skin warmed under the sun.

"Well, I'll be!" He stood, momentarily confused by the sweep of pleasure that ran through him. "Ronnie Baxter. I remember you."

Was that relief that flooded through her face? She hooked her thumbs in her cutoff belt loops and looked away. "I was sort of hoping that you really meant what you said—that you might have a job for me. I've kind of been looking..." She looked almost ashamed.

"Actually, yeah. I could really use someone to help with the store and who knows the equipment and can keep it clean and operational. Carol is helping out today, but what she knows about kayaks could fill a very small matchbook. The tour guides might hose off the salt water and sponge out the hull, but they're not good for much more. And given I'm out guiding a lot, I've had to close the shop, which means that I'm losing business from walk-in rentals. You interested?"Jeeze. He sounded like a school kid blurting out everything he knew.

But the wariness faded from her eyes and the shame disappeared in a flare of excitement. "Way interested."

"Perfect!" Because maybe this would give him the chance to understand why she wore suspicion like a second skin. It was something he could understand, given he carried an instinctive wariness, too. But what would make this lovely woman so uncertain? If he could understand, maybe he'd be able to sleep at night. And if he could sleep at night, maybe he could continue to hold together this nice little life of his. After five years of putting down roots, the thought of more running was exhausting. "So when can you start?"

She glanced up the hill to the parking lot that overlooked the water. "I—I could start now, but I've got Maddy in the car."

The shame was back in full force and she wouldn't meet his gaze.

"Hey. If Maddy's as well behaved here as she was at the beach the other day, she's welcome. Why don't you go get her and bring her down? Then I'll show you around here and you can give me a hand. If it works out, you're hired. If Maddy gets tired here, Mrs. Dermott up in the shop has a way with kids second to none."

She looked at him, her blue eyes so wide with gratitude it was like she couldn't believe, even though she desperately wanted to. That was the other thing written on her face and he was very good at reading people: desperation. If she hadn't been desperate, she wouldn't have been here.

Just what was going on with Ronnie Baxter?

Against his better judgment, he decided to find out.

CHAPTER 3

Two hours later Ronnie still felt like she had to pinch herself to wake up from the dream. The sun and breeze were warm. The ocean was blue. Maddy was busy with paper and colored pencils, drawing pictures of the boats and the seagulls. There'd even been a seal brave enough to come into the harbor and charm Maddy by popping its head above water to look at her. Seth had seemed to enjoy Maddy's presence, pointing out the difference between the glaucous-winged and the western gulls and showing her the community of starfish that hung out on the dock pilings.

Alone on the dock, because Seth had said he had a business meeting in the shop, Ronnie stood and eased her back from cleaning out the last of the kayaks, holding a wadded napkin like a trophy. It might seem like a kayak should stay pretty clean, but paddlers tracked in mud, leaves, and sand, and some idiots even went out of their way to harm a rental boat by doing things to jam the simple mechanisms that made the craft seaworthy.

"I got it, Maddy!" Her daughter looked up from her drawing and smiled the same million-watt smile that always made Ronnie's heart feel about to burst.

"I guess there's something to be said for being slim," Seth said.

Ronnie whirled around and found him, still in his sunglasses and ball cap, shorts, t-shirt, and Teva sandals, looking her appreciatively up and down. They obviously took business meetings differently here from Chicago. Jared wouldn't have been caught dead in that outfit. And here she'd been with her bum stuck in the air while she fought with the wad of napkin.

Where had he come from, anyway? She hadn't heard any footfall on the dock. For a big guy, he moved awfully quietly. Maddy hadn't said anything either and she was a pretty dependable chatterbox warning system.

The way Seth was looking at her, it was like he wanted to say something. Then he shook his head.

"So you managed to unjam the footrest and rudder line. Good. That's what I was fighting with when you arrived this morning." He took the neatly folded napkin from her and held it in his palm. "Are these people idiots, or what? Someone could have gotten in serious trouble if they went out in the kayak like this."

She nodded. "I always tell myself it's because people are jealous. They can't stay out there forever, so they don't want others to take their place. They want to be the only ones who paddled that kayak, who saw that scene, who has that memory. It makes them special, somehow."

"Maybe." Seth tipped his glasses at her so she almost glimpsed his eyes and a shiver ran through her.

"I think of them as the kind of idiots who shoot seals for fun." He shook his head. "Not good people."

He considered the racks of neatly stowed kayaks and the line of yellow and orange PFDs she'd hung to dry in the sun. "You've been busy."

Ronnie shrugged. "Things needed to be cleaned. The salt water and sun is hard on equipment."

He went over to inspect the gleaming kayaks and then sorted through the lifejackets. "All sorted by size..."

He turned back to her and she wasn't sure whether he was impressed or displeased. Darn sunglasses hid his gaze too well.

"I don't think I've had another employee who got as much done in such a short time." He stepped up to her and offered his hand. "You've proven yourself. You still want the job, it's yours."

It was the answer to a prayer! All she had to do was stretch the last of her savings a little farther and she and Maddy could have the life they wanted. A cozy little house. Warm breakfasts on cold winter mornings. A Christmas tree of lights, and most of all, safety. They would be safe together, all because this kind man had offered her a job. She could have thrown her arms around him and sobbed.

Instead she swallowed the emotions back and nodded, because once upon a time Jared had seemed like a good man, too.

"I'd like that. But until I get paid, I'm going to have to bring Maddy with me. Is that okay? Then I can look for childcare." She cringed, waiting for the hesitation and the shake of his head, "no". Having a job was such a fragile thing.

"That can work. If there's a problem, I'll let you know and give you a chance to find child care." He grinned at Maddy. "She seems like a really good kid."

"She's the best. She's been through a lot, but it seems to have made her stronger." Then she realized what she'd said. "It's been a long trip. A lot of moves. It's probably why she's so self-sufficient." And not seeing her mother battered on the floor. Not seeing her father with his fists ready. Not hiding in her bedroom and then creeping out with a towel to staunch her mother's bleeding lip for the fifth—sixth—seventh time.

"Listen, can you really do this? I mean can you really hire someone off the street like this? Don't you need to talk to someone? Your boss, maybe?"

That nice mouth of his split in a grin. "You're talking to him. The boss, I mean. I started the company five years ago when I came to the Sunshine Coast. It took off. The rest is history."

It was all happening so fast that it felt unreal, but the way he smiled at her, maybe it was the truth.

Through her daze she accepted his handshake and for a moment the strength and warmth of this very attractive man made her feel oddly safe for the first time in a very long while. His pleasant scent of sun-warmed male and sun block caught in her nose and held so her body melted a little and she was glad she couldn't see his eyes. That would have been way too intimate.

She slipped her hand free and looked away to the shed so that hopefully he couldn't read her thoughts. "So what else needs doing? If I'm on the payroll, I better make myself useful," she said, hoping to change the subject.

Seth seemed to shake himself as if he, too, had been affected by their touch. "There's a tour group headed out in half an hour. How about we get the boats ready."

Together they lifted kayaks down from the racks, untethered the rudders, and set paddles and PFDs out for each boat. In between, Seth found a coloring book of mermaids from his shop and made an instant hit with Maddy. Ronnie retrieved self-rescue equipment from the shed and put one flotation pad out for every five boats—three in this case. As she and Seth worked, they fell into a rhythm that, oddly, felt more like a dance the way each always seemed to be right where the other needed them to be. She felt Seth's gaze on her again.

"Is this okay? It's the way I used to do it," she said having put a paddle in each cockpit with the PFD slung over top.

Seth gave an appreciative nod. "Looks good to me. And just in time, too. Here they come."

She followed his gaze up the dock to where a gaggle of women clad in athletic shorts and matching t-shirts came toward them. Ronnie recognized the kind. The glint of too much gold and silver jewelry against tanned skin—not to mention diamonds—spoke of the wealthy sorority clans that had existed at university. Ronnie hadn't been part of it, though at one point she'd been asked to join—probably more because she was dating

Jared Douglas than for any merits of her own. Jared's sister and her friends had all been part of such things. These ones were likely out for an adventure that they could impress their friends with in their social media postings.

She went to look away, but a familiar face stopped her.

No way.

She was over three thousand miles from Chicago and Roberta Haze never left the windy city unless it was for New York or L.A. The woman had often opined that those were the only North American cities worth visiting, though she could force herself to visit Miami when the cold and snow hit the Midwest.

There was no way that city girl would be here, dressing like this... and yet...

There was the same sun-bright bob of yellow hair, the same haughty lift of chin, and the bobbing breasts that had cost her father plenty and that she liked to flaunt every chance she got. Even now, her t-shirt looked a size too small for her pushed-up balloons.

Ronnie caught herself. Now she was just being catty and she had other things to worry about because Roberta Haze *knew* her. Roberta Haze was still friends with Jared's sister and she would undoubtedly know about Jared's missing wife and child.

Ronnie had to get away, but the kayak business was at the end of the dock and there was nowhere to go except into the water. The water looked clean…

Who was she kidding? It was a damn good way to be noticed and it would leave Maddy unprotected. Trying to be casual, Ronnie spun around from Seth and his impending tour, crossed to Maddy, scooped her up and ducked them both into the equipment shed. It was a small building about fifteen feet by ten in one corner of the dock and crammed full of PFDs, paddles, hoses, and sundry equipment. She pressed into the shadows of the rear corner, next to a stack of old PFDs that stank of salt rot and old canvas. Now she was truly cornered. And if she refused to come out and help Seth with the tour, she might as well kiss her precious job goodbye before she'd ever had a chance to really get started.

"Mommy? What's going on?"

Ronnie held her finger to her lips, because even whispering, Maddy's clear voice carried. "Let's be really quiet and pretend like we don't want the people outside to hear us, 'kay?"

Maddy's open expression turned serious. "Is it—is it the bad man?"

Ronnie frowned. "The bad man?"

"The bad man that I dream about sometimes. He makes you cry."

Maddy's worried expression was enough to break Ronnie's heart. She pulled her baby into her chest. "No, baby, it's not the bad man. There'll be no bad man ever again, I promise." Not as long as she had breath in her lungs. "Now let's just stay quiet, okay?"

Maddy snuggled in and nodded as a figure blocked the sun-filled doorway.

Ronnie closed her eyes waiting for certain disaster.

"Hey. You okay?" Seth's voice was soft, even gentle, like someone would use with a frightened animal. Or a foolish woman.

She looked up at him and felt smaller than small as she nodded. "I just—there's someone out there—I can't let her see us." Please let him understand.

He glanced back at the doorway and sighed. "I sort of figured. I'll get them on their way. There's one of them asking if she'd just seen Ronnie Douglas. You know anyone by that name?"

She weakly shook her head. Please let him believe her.

"O—kay." He nodded. "I'll see what I can do."

He left them where they were. There was laughter and obvious flirting with the handsome tour guide, the soft splash of kayaks entering the water, and more laughter as the group, one by one, settled into their cockpits. Then there was a final soft splash, a knock on the wooden siding of the building as if signaling farewell, and then the retreating calls of people sliding away over the water.

Ronnie exhaled a breath she hadn't realized that she was holding and set Maddy down. She cautiously poked her head out the door. All clear, the brightly colored group of kayaks was leaving the harbor, leaving her time to escape.

This had been a mistake. The last thing she needed was to be working in the tourist industry. What better way was there to be seen? Nope, she needed to find something that would hide her in a back room.

Absently she picked up and straightened the debris of a tour group going out, coiling hoses, putting away PFDs that hadn't been the needed sizes. Maddy helped by picking up abandoned pop cans and putting them in the recycling. Then Ronnie carefully closed and locked the supply hut door and, with a sigh, headed with Maddy up to the car.

"Can we do that again tomorrow, Mommy? It was fun watching the seagulls and all the boats."

Ronnie settled Maddy in her car seat and climbed in behind the wheel. With regret, she shook her head. "I don't think so, sweetie. I think tomorrow we'll have to stay at the campground."

Or move on. Surely in the breadth and diversity of North America there had to be a place where Jared and his friends wouldn't find them.

CHAPTER 4

The next morning the sun poked its head above Keats Island, turning the blue water to azure just as it did most of the year. Last night the moon had been full and Seth had gone for a swim to sing the moon down. The quiet, steady rhythms of the sun, the moon and tides were the reasons he'd taken a chance and settled here after circumstances had forced him from his ancient homeland. After all, the quiet coves and rocky shores might not be as wild as the headlands that filled his memories, but they were welcoming and so were the people—at least so far.

Not for the first time, he glanced down the dock hoping for a glimpse of two blonde heads, one tall and one small. Surely he'd made it clear to Ronnie that she had the job, but clearly something had happened with the large group tour yesterday. The way she'd grabbed Maddy and huddled in the supply shed, she'd clearly been hiding. And then there'd been the fear on her face when he'd mentioned the name Ronnie Douglas. Clearly, like him, there were parts of her past she was hiding.

Let it go as just another bad experience with summer employees? He'd certainly had enough of them. He heaved in a sigh of briny air and finished hosing off the last of the kayaks. Maybe not as pristine and shiny as Ronnie had them yesterday, but good enough for the couple of regular kayakers who were taking out boats this morning. He set out equipment and then headed up the dock to the storefront.

Coastal Kayaks' shop was a small storefront across the lane from a steep, blackberry bramble-covered slope that led down to the water and the dock, with the kayak shed at the end. From the front window, between the kayaks on display, the gulls swooped over the early morning harbor and the water taxis headed out to Keats and Gambier islands. A seal lifted its head near the kayak dock.

"Sorry, buddy," he murmured as he let himself inside the shop. "No fish for you this morning. I've got other fish to fry." Like he hadn't asked Carol Dermott to come in because he'd figured that Ronnie would be here and could take care of things after he'd oriented her.

He couldn't very well call Carol now when she'd likely made plans. Which meant that he was going to be managing the shop and the kayaks himself. A bit of a stretch, but he'd done it before. He'd just close the shop when he was down on the pier. Still, it shouldn't be happening.

Damn personal radar had got that Ronnie all wrong. A person as desperate as she'd seemed would darn well be here for the job.

Unless something worse scared her off.

"Dammit."Because he wasn't going to let it go, was he? He was going to meddle in affairs that didn't concern him—again.

Hadn't he sworn off things like that after the trouble it had got him in before?

He couldn't risk losing everything again.

He toured the store—the shelves and displays of sunglass cords, compasses, and dry bags were all full. The fridge was stocked with bottled water. The ranks of PFDs and lifejackets offered all sizes. Middle-aged Carol Dermott might not be a kayaker herself, but she knew how to run a store. Even the restocking sheets were filled out and ready to file.

Which left him exactly nothing to do.

He hauled out a back issue of a kayaking magazine he'd been meaning to read and tried to amuse himself, but his mind kept straying to a certain strawberry blonde and the gasoline slick of fear in her eyes. Hadn't he said he wanted to understand her? Could he afford what it might cost if he did and tried to help her?

Because that was one of the things he *was* clear on. Ronnie Baxter—Douglas?—needed his help.

The two kayak groups arrived at nine o'clock sharp and took no time to get on the water. He watched them up and out of the harbor as the sun beat down on his shoulders. In the shelter of the harbor there was almost no wind, and the humidity and reflected sunlight from the water were high. It was the kind of day that he often left Carol in charge and escaped in a kayak alone to his favorite places to take a dip in the water. His skin itched at the prospect, but that would have to wait, too.

Leaving the pier, he jogged back to the shop, turned on the answering machine, turned over the shop sign to closed, and went out to his car. It was an older Jeep Cherokee that always smelled comfortably of salt gear and seaweed. Ronnie Baxter had started something when she spoke to him at Roberts Creek Campground. She'd confirmed his theory that there was some fate involved in their meeting when she'd shown up on his dock yesterday morning.

Swearing under his breath because he *didn't need this*—didn't need anything that could only last a year and a day—or cost him everything he'd built in the process. But he started the engine anyway and turned the vehicle northward.

It took only fifteen minutes to reach the turnoff to the provincial campground along the scenic Coastal Highway. Tall cedars and the typical brown-and-white provincial sign marked the entrance. He turned the Cherokee into the entrance toward the water and the pavement gave way to well-worn, potholed gravel and shadows. With his windows rolled down, the cool air under the trees and the sweet scent of cedar permeated the vehicle. Sunlight angled golden columns through the tree trunks to illuminate fern and huckleberry bushes or the long dead, moss-covered stump of a forest giant. He drove slowly along, checking out the campsites.

Most held behemoth-sized recreational vehicles complete with all the comforts of home. They leaked the bacon, egg, and coffee scents of late morning vacation brunches. With virtually no wind, from somewhere came the scent of campfire and a thin thread of smoke trailing through the woods. The campground road wound through the forested slope toward the glittering water glimpsed through the trees. He'd found himself at a dead end five times and was almost ready to give up when he spotted a beat-up Honda Civic next to a dome tent that gently collapsed as its supporting superstructure of bent poles was removed. A lone cooler sat on the picnic table and a pile of neatly rolled sleeping bags and other belongings were stacked beside the car. A blonde woman and a blonder child broke down the tent poles in preparation for rolling them inside the dome tent's nylon. Ronnie and Maddy. They were leaving.

He pulled the Cherokee in beside the Civic, a part of him wondering just why he was there. He owed nothing to this woman. He'd offered a job when she appeared to be able to fit a need he had in his business, that was all. She'd desperately seemed to want the job and then she had chosen not to show up.

Unstable, that was what he should be thinking. There were plenty of unstable people in the world today. Many were people with weapons. People he didn't want to be around.

But he was pretty sure something other than instability had Ronnie Baxter in this situation. Or Ronnie Douglas, if that was what her name was. Name changes he could understand.

He climbed out of the Cherokee and came around the vehicle. Ronnie stood like a startled deer with the tent bag in her hands. Maddy turned around from gathering tent pegs.

"Mr. Cullen! Hi!" Maddy's voice was welcoming, but Ronnie shushed her.

"Just gather the tent pegs. We need to be going if we're going to make the ferry," Ronnie said firmly as she finished deconstructing the tent frame and bent to roll the poles inside the tent.

Seth leaned his hip against the Cherokee's fender and crossed his arms as she rolled the tent just as efficiently as she cleaned and readied a kayak. She was a woman of spare movements. She studiously avoided looking in his direction. Maddy, on the other hand, finished her task and waved.

"I thought we had a deal. Instead, this morning you don't show up for work and leave me to deal with customers and get the boats ready alone. Not too professional," he said, letting his resentment show.

Ronnie glanced in his direction. "I'm sorry. I was pretty sure that you wouldn't want me back after yesterday's performance. You need an employee who won't run and hide from potential customers." She wrestled the rolled tent off the ground. "Maddy, hold the bag open for Mommy."

Maddy did and Ronnie slid the tent into the bag as if she'd done it a hundred times before. As if she'd been doing it for far too long. She stuffed in the small bag of pegs, carefully scanned the earth to make sure Maddy had retrieved all of them, and then brought the tent bag to the car to start loading.

"True," he said considering. "But I also need an employee who's good at their job. I've got to figure that there's a good reason when a good employee does something odd."

She straightened from piling sleeping bags into the little hatchback car, but didn't look at him and he found himself wanting to catch her arm, to lift her chin up so she couldn't ignore him.

"Some employees are only going to be trouble. You don't need me," she said.

He hauled himself up from the Cherokee and went to lift the cooler for her.

"I'm the employer. I know what I do and don't need." He stood close enough he could smell the baby powder she'd used that morning and the salt-sweet scent of woman. It evoked memories of another woman he'd tried to forget for far too many years. Gwyneth. Beloved and long dead. An old wound ached in his chest just below his heart.

"No one needs an employee that trouble follows." She tried to lift the cooler from his hands. "I really do need to get going if we're going to catch that ferry."

"So where are you going?" He didn't relinquish the cooler.

She looked at him then and her gaze held a combination of sadness and determination. "Somewhere where I can get a job where I don't have to deal with the public. Where my daughter doesn't have to hide in dark corners."

He let her take the cooler from him and then, against his better judgment, caught her shoulders. "Just what are you and Maddy hiding from, Ronnie? You're a good worker. You know kayaks, and I suspect you'll charm customers just like you've charmed me. I think you'd be a good addition to the business—if you decide to stay."

He heard himself saying the words when, dammit, he should just let her go. He hardly knew this woman and yet there was something about Ronnie Baxter that he'd been drawn to from the first moment he saw her.

She shook her head; her blonde locks an unruly tumble around her face. "I can't afford to stay. This campground's no bargain and Maddy needs better surroundings than carousing vacationers. Last night the next campsite was a drunken revel until two a.m."

"So rent a house or apartment."

"Right. I'll just do that." She stepped back and slammed the hatchback shut.

He suddenly understood: the pleasure in a tuna sandwich, the desperation in her gaze. This woman was proud and she was broke and she clearly was trying to hide from something while doing everything in her power to protect her child and be a good mother.

"Listen, I really get the sense you and Maddy like the coast. If it's a place you need, I-I happen to have a couple of spare rooms. I was thinking about maybe doing an Airbnb thing, but just never got around to it. If it would make it easier, you could camp out there until something you can afford comes along."

A flare of suspicion flashed across her gaze and he wanted to soothe it away. Hell, he wanted to touch her smooth cheek, take the vulnerable strength of her in his arms, and help her along.

Who was he kidding? There was something about her that attracted him in a far different, more primal way, and he hadn't felt that in a very long time. Maybe he should let her go. Maybe it would be safer—for both of them. His kind weren't known for sticking around for the long term.

But there was something about Ronnie and her daughter. Something that spoke of life and hope and endurance against all adversity. It was a struggle he could relate to. Something that made him want to remember, and perhaps relive, a happier time in his life. He glanced at Maddy, who was giggling as she gently prodded a furry caterpillar with a small stick. His son Caleb had never lived to see her age.

Maybe this time he could protect the people he cared about.

Or the protection wouldn't be necessary.

CHAPTER 5

The shadows of the trees placed dapples of shadow across Seth Cullen's face and the breadth of his shoulders. The cedar scent of the air was lost in the musky salt of his presence. Male through and through in a way that made Ronnie's toes want to curl, but that was a really good reason to back away and back away fast.

Her ancient Civic with its rusted fenders and dented rear bumper was a bastion of reality and she leaned against its solidity. She was a married woman. She was a fugitive who had stolen her child across the border. If she wanted to keep Maddy safe, they needed to keep moving; and if she really liked this man she wouldn't drag him into her troubles.

"That really is a kind offer, but..."

"But what? You have somewhere better to go? Somewhere better to hide? Listen, I've been there, all right? I've run from things—bad things—and if there's one thing I've learned, it's that eventually you have to make a stand if you want to have a life. Seems to me I'm trying to give you that chance. Or you can choose to run forever, but what kind of life is that for you or Maddy?"

It was a bolder, more personal appeal than she'd expected and to some degree it made sense, but... "You really don't need the baggage I bring, and Maddy is no concern of yours. She's *my* daughter."

"From what I can see, your baggage doesn't look like much." He grinned and lifted his chin at the Civic. "And as for Maddy, of course she's yours, but she's a pretty neat kid. I don't know too many who are attracted to tuna fish sandwiches and mermaids."

"It's not that baggage." And he wasn't that stupid. But he was a charmer. Hadn't her mother told her to watch out for that kind? Wasn't that what Jared had been—a charmer who charmed her right into being a virtual prisoner in her own home?

"So tell me."

There was a dare in his eyes and she wasn't playing, but the trouble was, she didn't want to leave this seaside community. Despite the run-in with Roberta Haze, the ferry ride from Vancouver had felt like it removed her from the danger of discovery and the slow, comfortable pace of living had met her needs completely. She folded her arms over her chest because, aside from the free ferry ride that would get them away from the Sunshine Coast, she really had no idea how she and Maddy would live.

"You've made a really generous offer, Seth, but my private life is my own and I'll not have you meddling in it." She thought a moment. "*If* I take you up on your offer, you have to promise not to ask me about my past again. And in exchange for you allowing us to use private rooms, I promise that we won't get underfoot or encroach on your space. We'll share the cost of heat and light, etc., until I get my own place."

His brows rose at her list and then he grinned. "Listen, there's nothing nefarious in my offer and sure you can share costs. I'd expect it—once you're on your feet. And in the meantime, you'll work at Coastal Kayak and make my life easier. Heck, it'll be easier just knowing that you're not living in a tent." He nodded at the rear of her hatchback.

"I'll have you know that that is a very good tent and has served us well."

"Okay. It's a very good tent that has served you well. Now, why don't you and Maddy climb in your car and follow me back to my place."

He waited while she herded Maddy into the car seat.

"Are we really leaving, Mommy?'Cause I like it here near the ocean." Maddy asked as Ronnie strapped her into her booster seat.

"I know you like it here, sweetie. But I thought we discussed this and that we have to go."

"Because of the money." Maddy sighed as if the world had fallen on her shoulders.

"Mr. Cullen has offered to let us stay at his place for a while. It will mean we'll have to share a kitchen with him and maybe a bathroom."

She could imagine dealing with the mess of an untidy man again, not to mention keeping Maddy out from under his feet. Jared had been okay when it had been just the two of them, but when Maddy was born, he seemed to return to his childhood when his doting mother had done everything for her only son. As if in competition with Maddy, he had contributed more than any toddler to the mess around the house and had done nothing to help clean up. Though he'd clearly loved to play with Maddy, he'd had no patience for how a young child could curtail the lifestyle he preferred. She'd come to realize that Jared's childhood had left him with few skills for parenting.

So what did she know about Seth? Did it matter? He was offering a free roof over their heads—as long as it didn't come with strings attached. She gave Maddy a tickle and Maddy squealed.

"The good thing about staying with Mr. Cullen is that we don't have to take the ferry away today."

"We don't?" Maddy's expression brightened. "We get to stay near the ocean? Yay! Yay, Mr. Cullen!" She leaned past Ronnie to call out to Seth, who lounged by his Cherokee.

"Yay, right back at you, Maddy."

My God, the man had the best smile. It seemed to totally fill him up and come from everywhere—except his eyes. She realized then that she had never seen them because he'd always worn sunglasses. There were lots of people for whom shades were an affectation. And there were people who needed glasses for some kind of eye condition. Not that it mattered.

Not that Seth Cullen seemed like the affectation type.

Pondering that, she climbed into her Civic, was relieved when it sputtered to life, and chugged out of the campground close on Seth's bumper. This was either the stupidest thing she'd ever done or the bravest. She couldn't figure out which.

Seth turned south, back toward Gibsons Landing, so he obviously lived closer to his business. *Nice, if you can get it.* She'd always found that any time she found work, it was usually located as far away as possible from any decent place she could afford to live. If the same paradox was true for Seth, then he was likely living in a hovel—men didn't necessarily realize these things—or he had money. And money usually meant men wanted something in exchange for helping a virtually destitute woman.

She'd have to be very careful around him.

He turned off the highway toward the water and then turned south again along a road with the water shimmering between the trees. He took a sharp right onto a driveway that led down a sloping path through cedars and pine and the twisting red-barked forms of arbutus trees. A low-slung wood-frame house nestled in a clearing that gave onto an unobstructed view of the ocean.

Ronnie slammed on the brakes.

A place with a view like that would cost a fortune. What the heck had she gotten herself into?

But Seth had pulled in by a two-car garage and was waving her in beside him. It would look pretty poor if she dropped her civic in reverse and skedaddled out of here.

She eased the car in beside him and turned the Civic off, then climbed out of her car. "Nice view," she said.

Seth shrugged. "I came by the property a while back. Prices were cheaper then."

He waited as she loosed Maddy and then hooked his head toward the door. "You probably want to see what you're getting yourself into before you decide to unload."

At least he understood she must have some reservations. Of course, that could also be how serial killers put their victims at ease; but she didn't get any dangerous vibe from him—not that she'd necessarily know one if she got one. And he'd been so good with Maddy. Of course, serial killers might be good at that, too.

"Oh, for God's sake, just go see," she said and shook herself. She followed after, holding Maddy's hand.

A solid stained oak door welcomed her under a small covered porch with a pair of man-sized rubber boots set neatly beside the door. At either end of the house, a high wooden fence ran off into the woods like long arms. Seth unlocked the door and ushered her and Maddy in.

They stepped inside to a large foyer with a floor of dark gray pebbles set in concrete that gleamed as if they were under clear water. An archway gave onto the front of the house where a wood-floored great room held low, comfortable, deep blue couches and chairs and a stone, floor-to-ceiling fireplace. An open ceiling exposed wood rafters and the steep roofline and broad windows exposed expansive views of a sleek concrete patio and, beyond, the woods, water, and the curved coastline of a rocky cove.

She led Maddy into the room and stopped. The faint scent of brine and cedar seemed to permeate the place, but otherwise it was clean. An array of hardcover books lay spine up on the coffee table as if Seth had been interrupted from reading. More books lined shelves on either side of the fireplace and were stacked on a table. In one corner stood what looked like an ancient, weathered cross with Celtic-looking knotted designs across the crossbar.

"This is—is amazing," she said and turned to look at Seth.

Still wearing his sunglasses, he leaned against the archway, his hands in his low-slung jeans pockets.

Why was he still wearing the glasses now that they were inside? A little alarm went off in her head.

"You were expecting a shack, maybe?" Seth asked.

"No. Well… maybe. I don't know, but not this." Not the sparkling clean of the great room, nor the array of what looked like well-thumbed books. She turned for another look out at the green-blue view. "You can't even see your neighbors."

He stepped into the room. "I don't have any—at least none close by. The property encloses the entire cove so I don't see anyone."

If that was the case, then why the fence? But complete privacy. A luxury, or was he trying to hide something, like he seemed to hide his eyes behind his sunglasses? She felt nervous and tightened her hold on Maddy's hand. She'd been really stupid doing this, especially with Maddy. Maybe all the things Jared said about her were true. Maybe she wasn't a good mother when it came to keeping Maddy safe.

She was just about to take Maddy and leave—if she hurried she might still make the ferry—when a large cat with golden ears and a long, ringed tail sauntered across the yard to flake out on the patio just in front of the sliding glass doors. It had a gold-, brown-,and black-marbled coat, white chin, and black kohl-type markings around golden eyes.

"Mommy, look!" Maddy ripped her hand away and tore away to the window. "What kind of kitty is that?"

Ronnie followed her daughter and peered doubtfully out at the cat. "That's no ordinary kitty, sweetie. That looks like—a small leopard?" She shot a questioning glance in Seth's direction as he joined them.

"Nope. Just looks like one. He's a Bengal, at least that's what the vet tells me. He walked in here one day and has apparently decided to stay. Roscoe and I have an agreement. I acknowledge him as royalty and he graces me with his presence."

Ronnie shook her head. "But he's so big. There's no way I could allow Maddy to play outside. This won't work at all."

Seth caught her arm and a warm tingle ran through her.

"Hold on, Ronnie. It's different than you think." He clicked something on the wide glass wall and suddenly it began to move, sliding to one side so a gust of sun-warmed ocean air filled the room. Roscoe turned an unperturbed golden gaze on them, then looked back to the ocean.

"He—he looks like a king surveilling his domain," Ronnie said.

"He's all of that, and more, aren't you, Roscoe?" Seth knelt beside the cat and buried his hand in thick, plush fur, scratching Roscoe's neck. "When he arrived he wasn't much more than a kitten, but fiercely independent. He'd got himself tangled in a fisherman's line that had come ashore and had swallowed down a bunch of it when he was trying to free himself. He was in pretty bad shape when I rescued him. A friend who's a vet gave me a hand and I nursed him back to health. He's stayed with me here, ever since."

He looked up at her and she wished she could see his eyes, because her trust was wavering.

"Bengals are domestic cats, you know. Have been for a number of generations."

A deep rumbling purr came from the cat and he turned an apparently adoring gaze up at Seth.

"Maddy can pat him, if you like."

He and Maddy practically oozed the need for her approval. Darn it, she wanted to see his eyes so she knew she could trust him They'd be nice eyes, she was sure.

"Can I, Mommy? Please?" Maddy had been mad for cats since she was very little. It was one of Ronnie's promises to herself that when they had a home, she'd get Maddy a kitten.

But Ronnie held firm against Maddy's tugs for freedom. If something happened to Maddy, there'd be no forgiving herself. But the cat was a domestic, according to Seth...

"It's really okay. See?" Seth ran his hand down Roscoe's side and darned if the cat didn't almost roll over to expose his belly for a rub.

"Let me try it first, sweetie. It's no big deal if I get scratched."

She set Maddy behind her and crouched down beside Seth. The big cat had a distinctive clean fur and fresh air scent that was actually pleasant. Cautiously she reached out a hand.

Roscoe righted himself and reached out his nose.

"Just let him sniff you."

She did. And then the big cat lifted his head and placed it into her palm in a clear request that she rub his chin. She did and that great golden gaze went to half-mast as the cat's purr rumbled.

All her reservations faded away as the vibration of the purr filled her hand like the softness of the fur. She glanced at Seth and he nodded.

"Come here, Maddy. Slowly!" when Maddy darted forward.

Maddy slowed to a creeping crawl and then eased in between them to kneel beside Roscoe. "He's so pretty. Why did you name him Roscoe?" she carefully held out a hand for the cat to sniff.

Roscoe lifted his head from Ronnie's hand and turned to her daughter. Sniffed again, gave an audible sigh, and dropped his head right into Maddy's lap.

Maddy gave a little yip of delight and stroked Roscoe's golden ears. The breeze ruffled the cat's fur and

Maddy's blonde hair, and the peace and magic of the moment caught in Ronnie's chest. She almost couldn't breathe. Almost wanted to cry. Then something moved in the woods beyond the patio and Roscoe abandoned them and his spot of sun and trotted into the woods almost as if he was on patrol. His gold-black pelt melted into the shadows as if he was never there.

"That was—something," she said, rocking back on her heels and then standing. "I think we should thank Mr. Cullen for introducing us to Roscoe, don't you, Maddy?"

They did and then he showed them the kitchen—well equipped with all the modern conveniences, and just beyond the kitchen, the connecting rooms—two bedrooms and a shared Jack and Jill bathroom that would serve as their space, all pleasantly decorated in tropical sea blue. When they returned to the great room, Roscoe was back sunning himself.

"So why did you name him Roscoe, Mr. Cullen?" Maddy asked, kneeling beside the cat again.

"Well, If ya must know, it was because he was such a little scrapper as a kitten and I thought the name would keep him grounded. A cat like that could get very conceited."

Ronnie had to smile at the silly explanation, but Maddy nodded sagely.

Looking around the room, Ronnie appreciated the place and the man with a new light. If nothing else, Seth Cullen had good taste. But he was also someone who had rescued a wild kitten and who still had the cat's trust and respect.

Surely he was someone she could trust, too. At least she could reserve judgment.

Chapter 6

Seth looked out the front window of the Coastal Kayak store. The sun had fallen westward enough that the bright red of the pier was now stained with amber and the brightly painted houseboats tinted yellow. The restaurant and bar crowd would be gathering at the restaurants down the street though he could not hear them in the shop. In the harbor, the last kayaking group of the day was going out with a guide who would lock up and make sure the kayaks were all put to bed when they returned.

On the Coast Kayak dock, Ronnie waved them on their way, her red-gold hair turned coppery in the light. Maddy's head was a golden coin bent over her coloring book at the picnic table. The child had been at it all day, even though her crayons had turned soft in the sun. The small party of kayaks left the harbor and Ronnie got busy, hosing off the dock, tidying the floatation devices, and locking everything away. She tugged the padlock on the hasp and gave a nod that made Seth smile.

There was something so, well, determined in practically everything Ronnie did. As if she had something to prove—to herself and to the world. The funny thing was that all you had to do was meet Ronnie and you knew she was competent. Even the episode yesterday hiding in the shed had just raised more questions, but not about her competence.

She glanced up at the shop as if she felt his regard and maybe there was a smile on her face as if she thought of him, too.

Seth shook his head in disgust and forced himself back to the till. He was living in a flipping fairy tale if he thought she was thinking of him with anything akin to affection. The second day at Coastal Kayak had gone well enough, even if he kept catching Ronnie's suspicious glances at him throughout the day. Someone had seriously messed with this woman and the protective way she mothered Maddy said it was more—far more— than a simple man-woman thing. Someone had scared Ronnie enough that she acted as if she might never trust again.

And of course he'd been the damned fool who had dragged her out her car and into his home.

He cashed out the receipts and felt the usual satisfaction he got when he considered a good day's take. If the business kept growing like this, he might have to consider opening a second site—at least for the summer. Maybe have a mobile service that would operate at Roberts Creek or Sechelt. That was the thing about business: once you stabilized the first fledgling operation, it could grow and thrive and become more as he built his relationship with the community.

And that was the only relationship he was going to build at the moment. A solid membership on the Chamber of Commerce and the Downtown Business Association, and that was enough for him. He had a place in the world again and this time he was going to keep it.

The bell over the door jingled and a breathless Maddy shoved inside. "I beat Mommy."

She gave a satisfying nod. "Mommy said it was time to go home and I said I'd race her up to the store. I won."

"So you did." Seth tucked the receipts in the bank bag as the door jingled again and Ronnie stepped in.

"Too early? I've got everything down at the water put away and locked up. The guide just has to hose off her three boats, stash her equipment, and lock the gate behind her when she leaves."

The ocean wind had tossed her rich hair around her face and the sun had placed a glow on her skin that still couldn't banish a certain pallor that seemed to come from within. Worry.

"You're right on time. You did good today, but then I figured you would. It gave me time to take care of things up here. I've been remiss leaving everything to Carol this season—it's just gotten that busy."

He tucked the bag under one arm and hiked a kicking, squealing Maddy under the other. "Shall we go? I think I've got everything."

Ronnie glanced up at him and for once her suspicion let go to reveal a wonderful smile—with dimples, no less. Now he knew where Maddy got them from.

"Mommy! He'd tickling! Make him put me down!" Maddy's giggles were infectious and Ronnie's smile broadened.

She shook her head. "You had to beat me up to the store. You pay the price." She pulled the door open and ushered Seth and his protesting passenger past. Outside he tossed Maddy over his shoulder and bounded up the stairs to the parking lot where his jeep was parked. Ronnie followed behind.

At home he poured Maddy an orange juice and Ronnie and himself a glass of wine as he pulled meat and buns from the freezer. He could feel Ronnie's gaze on him, watching and waiting as if for something untoward to happen.

"Hamburgers okay?"

He glanced at her and found her watching. She glanced away, back to the patio where Maddy was stalking Roscoe. Every time she settled down to pat the big cat, he'd shift position as if he was testing her resolve to be his friend.

Ronnie looked back at him. "I swear your cat is training my daughter. Who would have thunk it, obedience training from a cat?" She grinned and this time it was a little broader, a little sweeter, and Seth's heart went bump-bump.

No way in hell. He looked down at the meat he held. "Hamburgers?"

"Oh, yeah. Sure. We eat just about anything. Maddy loves hamburgers."

"As long as it's not peanut butter and jelly sandwiches, I'm good, I take it."

He said it casually, but Ronnie froze.

"I'm sorry," she said, but a chill was in her voice. "We were supposed to stop at the store so that I could buy the groceries for dinner. Let me get you the money."

She headed for the back bedroom next to Maddy's room.

"Hey! Hey! That's not why I asked!" He caught her arm before she could head down the hall. "I was planning on hamburgers myself. There's enough here for three." Note to self: Ronnie Baxter did not like any reference to her financial situation. He supposed he could understand. Shame was a powerful emotion and not being able to give her daughter everything she wanted clearly bothered Ronnie.

She looked up at him, suspicion-shame-anger warring on her face. Finally she sighed and quit resisting his hold. "I'm sorry. I seem to be doing a heck of a lot of reacting these days and not in a good way. But let me buy the groceries tomorrow. Please. You've done enough for us."

The woman had pride and he would be damned if he would rob her of that.

"Deal." He nodded. "Now while I get the meat ready, maybe you can slice tomato and shred lettuce and get the buns ready."

"Deal." She gave a quick grin and then, in that competent way of hers, she rummaged in the fridge and then found cutting implements. Surprisingly, she seemed to find everything she needed as if she'd worked in his kitchen for years.

Soon, with Maddy's help, the table was set with ketchup, relish, mayo and mustard; the barbeque was sizzling with hamburger juices; and Ronnie had taken the initiative to whip up some potato salad using baby potatoes, frozen peas, and some artichokes and tarragon she found in his fridge. She'd seemed surprised he had such things. Yup. That was him. A veritable renaissance man.

If she only knew.

They sat down to dinner as the setting sun was lacing golden fingers over the cove. The trees glowed on the bluff on the far side of the water. An arbutus tree's red bark burned russet. Angled sunlight caught Ronnie's face.

She frowned at him; he wasn't sure why.

Maddy was eyeing the grilled patties on the platter and the bun on her plate. As if she was doing the math, she opened her mouth wide, then closed it again. Her lower lip quivered.

"Mommy? I'm not sure I can eat one of these big burgers." She looked up at her mother, clearly distressed. "They smell really good."

Ronnie focused on her daughter and the tension and disapproval he'd sensed disappeared. "It's okay, sweetie. If it's too big, we can always cut it into little pieces that you can eat with the fork."

"Sacrilege!" Seth said in mock horror. "You will not eat this perfectly good burger with a fork, young lady." He leaned down until his face was even with Maddy's across the table. "I will demonstrate the secrets to eating a big burger, but you have to watch closely and copy everything I do. Can you do that?"

Maddy checked with Ronnie, who had sat back with her arms across her chest and a wait-and-see attitude. She nodded.

"So. To make the very best burger, you have to put the right things on it. Are you a ketchup or a mustard girl?" he asked.

"Can I have both?" Maddy asked.

"Of course! Girl after my own heart." He helped her slather mustard and ketchup on her bun, agreed wholeheartedly with her that relish had no place on a hamburger, and then let her choose the hamburger patty she wanted.

"That's pretty big." Maddy shook her head.

"We're not finished yet. Do you like lettuce and tomato?"

"Lettuce, please."

He passed the tray to her, catching a small smile from Ronnie as she watched the proceedings.

Maddy placed a small poof of shredded lettuce on top of the patty. Seth topped his own lettuce with sliced tomato.

"Okay. Now comes the tricky part. You might need to get up on your knees on your chair."

Ronnie looked at him sideways, but she didn't get in the way of the bad manners he was teaching.

"Now you can only do this at home, you understand, because if you do it at a restaurant, you give away the secret process."

Maddy nodded.

"Put the top bun on the burger." Maddy followed his example, her bun balanced precariously on the poof of lettuce. "Now comes the secret method."

He laced his fingers together and did stretches over his head and side to side. Giggling, Maddy copied him and Ronnie shook her head and smiled.

"Ready?"

"Ready!" Maddy said.

"Oh, so ready," Ronnie chimed in dryly.

"Hey! You got to get into the spirit."

He placed his hands on top of each other on top of the burger and pressed down.

Maddy did the same, sending a stream of ketchupy hamburger juice oozing out the side of her burger.

"Look, Mommy! It worked! It's smaller, so maybe I can bite it." Maddy said. She went to copy Seth, who picked up his burger and took a big bite.

"Hold on a moment, sweetie. Let's get you prepared for this," Ronnie said and took two napkins and tucked them in Maddy's shirt collar. "I have a feeling that if you didn't need a bath before, you're going to now."

Maddy picked up the burger and took a bite, the meat escaping out the back of the bun until Ronnie fixed it for her.

"This is the best burger ever, Mommy. You should watch what Mr. Cullen did so we can have them again." Maddy chewed down and Ronnie glanced in Seth's direction. Then she put together her burger and nibbled at it as if she wasn't hungry.

Maddy giggled through the meal, talking about Roscoe and the things she'd seen at the harbor. Ronnie was mostly silent, apparently content to eat her food and clean up Maddy's mess, because Maddy's burger was a disaster with the bun gradually disintegrating and her hands covered in ketchup and mustard. When Maddy had had enough, she sat back in her chair and yawned.

"I think someone has had a full day." Ronnie said. "I hope you don't mind, but it's almost Maddy's bedtime and I want her to have a bath first. Leave the dishes. I'll do them when I'm done."

She slid her chair back and caught Maddy's hand, but Maddy slid off her chair and came around the table. "Thank you for the burger, Mr. Cullen. It was really good and I'll remember your secret method."

"Just remember to do the stretches. It always helps," Seth said.

Maddy nodded wisely and left.

Seth watched them go and finished the last of his burger, old memories flooding back of his family. Of the games he'd played with his infant son. Of another woman, lost long ago. In some ways Ronnie reminded him of her. Maybe it was the copper tint to her hair or the stiff-necked pride that seemed to underpin everything Ronnie did.

Either way, there was no getting away from the potential attraction he felt. But it was just potential. He'd never let it be more than that.

§

The bathroom of creamy white tiles and marble counters was awash with steam and water. Steam filled the air. The water, though, had slopped over the tub top as Maddy kept practicing the kneel and press position, pressing down on soapsuds with her rosy, little-girl hands.

"See, Mommy. I think I've got it right now. I'll do much better next time." Maddy smiling winningly up at her, her blonde hair flattened against her scalp from an immersion under the water like the mermaids in Maddy's coloring book. A gift from the all-too-charming Seth Cullen.

Maddy clearly like him. But the darn man was doing nothing but teaching her daughter poor manners. First keeping his darned sunglasses on *in the house* and after the sun was mostly down, and *then* teaching Maddy whatever it was he'd taught her at dinner. Didn't he realize that children were a sponge picking up everything around them?

Maddy did another kneel-and-press performance, sending more water across the floor.

"Okay. You are officially the best kneel-and-press person I know. Time to get out of the tub and get some sleep. We have another busy day tomorrow." Depending on how tonight goes. If Seth Cullen tried anything they would be out of here so fast...

She helped Maddy out of the tub and wrapped her in a luxuriously thick navy blue towel.

Of course, for all she knew, Seth could be an axe murderer and they could both be dead in the morning.

Heart racing even though she knew she was a fool, she left Maddy toweling her hair and went out to the bedroom doors. Locks were on both of them.

That was something, at least.

Back with Maddy, Ronnie finished toweling Maddy's hair dry and combed out the long, almost silver strands until she had a mass of gold in her hands. Pink p.j.s on, Maddy climbed into the bed in the most luxurious room she'd ever known. But then kids didn't notice things like that.

Ronnie tucked the covers up around her and settled on the edge of the bed. "You going to be okay in here by yourself?"

Maddy nodded. "I like it here, Mommy. Roscoe is neat and Mr. Cullen is nice. And this room is way better than our tent, plus we have a real bathroom."

So maybe children did notice.

She ran a finger down Maddy's smooth cheek, then tapped her nose and chucked her chin before leaning in to kiss her cheek. "I love you so much, sweetie. But we can only stay here a short time—just until we get our own place. So don't get too attached to Roscoe—or Mr. Cullen. Okay?"

Maddy nodded and wrapped her arms around Ronnie's neck. "It's okay, Mommy. We're safe here."

Ronnie pulled back and looked down at her daughter. "What makes you say that, sweetie?"

Maddy shrugged. "I don't know. It just feels safe. Maybe it's Mr. Cullen. The way he looks at you."

A shiver ran down Ronnie's back. There was no way that Maddy could have seen anything like that on Seth Cullen's face, because he was always in those stupid sunglasses.

"Well, just remember what I said. We won't be here forever. We'll have our own place. Our own life. Our own cat."

"A kitten?"

"Yes, Maddy. A kitten." Ronnie smoothed Maddy's hair and stood, then leaned down to plant a kiss on her forehead. "Now sleep. Sleepyheads don't get to come to the harbor or play with Roscoe in the morning."

At the room's door, she paused. Maddy's eyes were already closed. Oh, to be that young again and to be so trusting. It was something Ronnie doubted she would ever find again.

After mopping up the bathroom, she went out to the kitchen to find the dishwasher humming and the kitchen clean. Seth looked up at her from the couch where he was reading. Soft Celtic music played in the background from unseen speakers, and a real wood fire burned in the fireplace.

For a moment she was ashamed that she hadn't at least cleaned up after the meal. He probably waited and then just assumed that she was avoiding the task. Then she got angry. He couldn't even allow her that much self-respect. Oh, no, Mr. Seth Cullen had to have her even more beholden to him, and now he practically had his living room set up for seduction. Heck, he was even sipping a glass of white wine.

With a shake of her head she avoided confrontation and went outside onto the stone patio.

The light was failing. She'd missed what she assumed must have been a glorious sunset during Maddy's bath. Now faint fingers of gold and red were slowly fading away into dusk. The trees were tall and dark and creaking in a new wind off the water. From the cove came the sound of waves falling against the shore. The air had turned deliciously cool after the heat of the kayak dock all day. She hugged herself and closed her eyes, inhaling the cedar and salt scent, letting it ease the tension from her shoulders.

She knew Seth was there long before he said anything. It was as if the night parted around him, leaving behind a stillness. The wind carried his scent of man-musk, cedar, and brine.

"I'm sorry," she said, sighing. "I should have done the dishes. I really wasn't avoiding it."

"There's nothing to be sorry for." He stepped up beside her, the last dregs of sunset somehow finding his face through the trees. "They needed doing and you were obviously busy putting Maddy to bed."

"Putting the mermaid with the secret hamburger-squashing method to bed. That required a little more effort. You should have seen the bathroom from all the practicing."

"I guess I'm the one who should apologize," he said and she felt the radiance of his warmth and was too aware of the size and strength of him. For a moment she was afraid, but Seth acted the perfect gentleman with his hands shoved in his shorts pockets.

"For a moment there I was jealous that you were having so much fun with Maddy." It was a half-truth, Seth Cullen didn't need to know the rest.

Out of the corner of her eye she caught the shake of his head. "You've got nothing to worry about. She's a great kid and she loves you to pieces."

Ronnie nodded. "Thanks. I guess sometimes I think that I'm never enough for her. Can never do enough, be enough, teach her the right things."

"Whoa." He said is softly. "Maybe you need to believe in yourself more. From what I've seen, you're a pretty great mother."

She shook her head. "You've known me for two days. Maybe three. There are people who know me better who wouldn't agree with you." She turned to him then. "Thank you for everything, Seth. You really have done too much. I don't know how or if I will ever be able to repay you, but I will try."

His sunglasses blocked her ability to read his expression, but he stood close, one hand raised as if he was about to say something. Too close. She backed away a step. "It's been a good day, but I'd better hit the sack if I'm going to do it again tomorrow. 'Night."

She didn't wait for whatever it was that he was going to say. Instead she turned to the house and didn't glance back until she was in the hallway. Through the open patio door, Seth still stood there, a darker shadow in the night air; and for a moment she was struck by a sense of loneliness as if Seth Cullen was the last of his kind, a unicorn that she wanted to comfort.

A foolish thought.

Both the unicorn and the comfort.

CHAPTER 7

Roscoe at his side, Seth nursed his first coffee of the day in an old Adirondack chair on his house's stone front patio and watched the dawn creep into the sky. The morning was lovely with the salmon steaks of sunrise filling the day with promise, except that he was too aware of the woman sleeping in the house behind him. He'd been too aware of her since before she even set foot on the Sunshine Coast. He'd been swimming when he first became aware of her and had been pulled off course as if she was a new magnetic north for him.

And that couldn't be. She was just a woman in distress. He'd made a life here. He didn't want to leave it, and he would have to if he got involved. The old curse was still potent, even after all these years.

He wore only his swimming trunks, for he'd already had his daily swim with the first hint of the new day. First came the amber glow above the trees that framed the eastern arm of the cove. Then came beams of light radiating up to paint the undersides of the clouds gold. Then came the glorious light that caught in the tops of the trees and gradually worked its way down to the water as the sun rose. In turn, the waves changed from gray to blue to turquoise as the tide came in and returned his strength. Change, waxing and waning, that was the only rule to life. Constant change from one moment to the next. But his sense of direction was still horribly awry.

What was happening to him?

Her first night here and he'd nearly broken down and told her his own story just to prove that she wasn't the failure she seemed to think she was. At the last minute he'd caught himself because Ronnie Baxter was clearly guarded and he knew she would never believe anything like his wild story. Telling her his tale would be about the best way he could think of to chase her away. He sighed.

So he'd let her leave him with so many things unsaid. A chance to comfort her, lost.

A week after the move-in and his house had fallen into a new kind of rhythm. It wasn't quite the rhythm he'd always lived by—up with the dawn, energy waxing and waning with the tides, ready to bed down with the falling sun—but having the rhythms of a child in the house was definitely worth something. And Ronnie.

Their bright hair and laughter. The way the light filled their eyes and how it took so little to please them. Just yesterday he'd spotted a perfect forget-me-not caught between the lawn and the base of the forest. The sun through the trees had spotlighted its robin's-eggshell blue against the grass and both Ronnie and Maddy had stood in awe of its perfection. It had seemed like a sign that they were relaxing—or at least Ronnie was. Maddy had trusted him right from the start. It was one of the wonders of children, that capacity to trust.

He sipped his coffee and enjoyed the dark chicory flavor and the hint of brine absorbed from the weeks in transit in sacks in a ship's hold. Coffee was a relatively newly acquired taste, but he'd quickly become as addicted as the people around him and had found the best beans from a small bean roaster firm fifteen minutes up the coast. It was nice, as well, to have the breeze full on his face, his sunglasses perched for a time on the crown of his head.

Time was, he wouldn't have worn the glasses, but he'd found that his eyes conveyed an inhuman strangeness that most people were repulsed by. The sunglasses were a way to avoid that reaction and to narrow the gap between himself and humans.

He glanced back at the still-quiet house—even Ronnie wasn't quite the early riser he was and Maddy, though an early riser, couldn't equal him either. Who was he kidding? The sunglasses had become a way to not scare Ronnie and to keep her close. She'd been nervous enough about accepting his offer. When she'd asked why he always wore them, he'd fibbed and said it was for a sensitive eye condition. Not good to start a relationship with a lie.

Lies had a habit of multiplying. He'd heard Ronnie repeat his story when she explained to Maddy that it was not generally considered polite to wear sunglasses in the house or after dark.

But then who said this was a relationship?

Ronnie was lovely, a red-gold-bronze goddess of a woman, but their developing friendship could never be something more. He was settled here. Anything more with Ronnie would mean he would lose not only her, but everything else he held dear.

So they would remain friends and he would help her recover from whatever had left her hiding on the coast. Then he would let her go.

Roscoe lifted his head, his nostrils working as he scented the wind. In one smooth movement, he was on his feet peering toward the eastward edge of the cove. A bristling ruff of fur rose down his spine and his ears went back. A rumbling growl filled the morning.

Seth leapt to his feet and stood beside the cat. He inhaled, letting his other senses take in the morning. Sharper hearing allowed him to hear the whisper of pebbles along the shore, the lap of water in small tidal pools as they relinquished themselves to the incoming tides.

A sharp crack of a distant twig in the forest screamed of a careless footfall.

No animal would make such noise.

Someone was there. Someone coming for him? The little hairs rose on the back of his neck.

He set down his coffee cup as Roscoe loped into the brush. Seth followed.

Slick leaves of rhododendron and young arbutus slapped against his skin. Thorn brush and blackberry brambles with moon-white blossoms tore at him, but he ducked away, sleeking through the forest like he would through the sea.

The ground, soft from millennia of fallen cedar and pine needles, swallowed his footfall as he climbed to the ridge that ran the length of the eastern edge of the cove. Here and there, smooth granite shrugged out of the soil and grew a thick pelt of sphagnum moss. Roscoe smoothed over the rocks like a gold-black ghost. Seth, still barefoot, dug in with his toes as he neared the high point on the ridge.

Roscoe crouched immobile beneath a tree, his tail thrashing unhappily.

Seth knelt beside him and inhaled cigarette smoke and men's floral cologne that overpowered the natural cedar and brine. Seth went down on his belly and matched Roscoe's low view of the intruders on his land.

Two sets of black-booted feet. Two sets of legs in camouflage fatigues. He worked his gaze up through the branches and brush between the intruders and himself. Both were brawny men with the weathered faces of years on the ocean. One held a pair of binoculars to his eyes and used them to scan the cove and then locked in one place.

"Seth?" Ronnie's call echoed through the forest.

The man with the binoculars dropped his glasses and the two men spoke in hushed voices. Then they melted away eastward down the ridge toward the coastline that separated Seth's cove from the town of Gibsons. He stood and listened to their footfall down the ridge to the water. The grumble of a small outboard motor said how they'd got here. He pushed through the last of the brush to watch them go, a silver inflatable zodiac buzzing southeastward toward the harbor. He'd have to ask around to learn who they were.

When they'd gone around a curve in the coastline, he turned back to the view of his cove. Nestled amongst the trees, the broad front windows of his house glinted in the morning sun. In plain view, Ronnie and Maddy were outside, Maddy sipping cocoa—her usual morning drink—and coloring in her mermaid book, and Ronnie slumped in the second Adirondack chair, her hair aflame in the sunshine. Then Ronnie got up and went inside to the kitchen window.

Seth's skin prickled in concern as he checked the empty shoreline behind him again.

Were these men a sign that whatever Ronnie feared had finally found her, or had his long-lost enemies finally found him?

§

Ronnie was just finished scrambling some eggs for the three of them when Seth came in through the open patio door. He brought Maddy with him, though she'd been happily coloring in the morning sunlight. Then he abruptly closed the door, blocking the lovely ocean breeze.

"Hey. I was enjoying the fresh air!" she said, basking in the sunny warmth through the windows of the ocean-blue kitchen. She couldn't think of anything better than being able to spend her life in a room like this—even if this was just a borrowed moment in a kitchen owned by someone else. She could dream, couldn't she?

"What a glorious morning!" she continued as she sprinkled some cheese over the eggs, and oozy goodness ensued—Maddy's favorite breakfast. "That Irish group sure got lucky considering the weather reports were all for rain. I guess I'll just have to learn to listen to you when you tell me they're wrong." With the frying pan of fresh eggs in hand, she turned, grinning, to the table she'd already set.

And caught sight of Seth's expression. Lips in a compressed line, his shoulders square and his jaw working. She knew the signs—Jared had the same dangerous look whenever something wasn't quite to his liking.

Feeling cornered, her mind whirled through everything she'd done, said, been since she and Maddy arrived. She looked down at the eggs. It had to be her. She'd thought things were going pretty well. In fact, there were times after a long day when Seth and she made dinner for the three of them that it felt like the happy family she'd always dreamed of having. Seth was—well—he was Seth. Strange and distant in some ways and yet so familiar and decent in another—almost as if he was someone her heart knew even though her brain didn't.

She set the frying pan down. "If you want something other than eggs, I can..."

Once upon a time she'd told herself that she and Jared were that happy family. Of course, she'd been kidding herself even early in their relationship. And now she was doing it again. She wasn't married to this man. She was a guest in his home—his tenant beholden to him for her job and for the roof over her and her child's head.

She gripped the edge of the granite counter, dread filling her gut, the scent of scrambled eggs unsteadying her stomach. "What's wrong?"

With his hands on Maddy's shoulders, he moved her daughter to the couch and sat her down, then closed the blinds on the window behind her and knelt before her. "You stay here. Do not—I repeat, *do not*—go outside until I'm back, do you hear?"

Maddy nodded at him, her eyes carrying a seriousness that no four-year-old should ever have. Ronnie had to bite her tongue to stop herself from interceding, but the expression on his face said there'd be no denying him.

He crossed the room to Ronnie. "We need to talk." He hooked his head back to the hall that led to her and Maddy's bedrooms.

Suddenly not hungry, she dutifully followed until he turned to confront her.

"What are you running from—or who?" His expression was deadly serious.

She shook her head. "I told you before, my personal history is none of your business."

He loomed over her and suddenly his superior height made her feel vulnerable. She backed a step and went to return to the kitchen.

Seth caught her wrist and tugged her back to him. "That was before I caught two men spying on my home."

She froze and her heart stopped in her chest. It couldn't be. It just couldn't be. There was no way Jared could track her so far so fast. She couldn't breathe and looked up into her reflection in Seth's damned sunglasses, unable to read anything in his hidden eyes, then looked away feeling weak and helpless. She needed to pack. She and Maddy needed to get out of here as soon as they could. It wouldn't take much. She hadn't even fully unpacked their suitcases into the dressers. Her car—it was working well enough since Seth spent some time on it.

She tugged away and sighed, feeling tired and old and oh-so-cold. From the living room, Maddy was singing to herself. She clearly liked it here, and Seth and Roscoe.

"I'm sorry. I told you that you didn't want to be involved. Maddy and I'll pack up and go right after breakfast, okay?"

"Dammit, Ronnie." He kept his voice low against Maddy hearing. "That's not what I want. I need to know what's going on, so I can figure out who those men are. There's—there's a chance this isn't about you at all."

It took a moment to process what he was saying. "They might not be after Maddy and me? Why? Are they after you?"

He gave a grim little shake of his head. "We all have our secrets, don't we?"

"So, what? I tell you mine and you'll tell me yours?" she asked.

He almost looked like he was considering it, but then he shook his head. "They don't know that I saw them, but I need to know what kind of danger you're in if I'm going to protect you."

"Pro—protect me?" Since when had anyone ever protected her? Keeping them safe was a burden she carried alone out of necessity. There was no one else she could trust. She swallowed and shook her head. "How can I trust you to do that, when you don't even trust me enough to uncover your eyes."

He went statue still.

She nodded. "That's what I thought. It won't take long for me to pack." She stepped past him to her bedroom and tossed her small bag on the bed. There wasn't much—just the shorts, t-shirts, bathing suits, and light sweaters one might expect of someone going to Disneyworld. She pulled underwear out of the sleek black dresser and tossed them beside her half-filled bag.

Dammit, why did she feel like her life was ending again? Why did she feel like crying this time? She'd left everything she knew in Chicago and hadn't cried then.

"Ronnie, don't." Seth had come up behind her and rested his fingers lightly on her shoulders. "Don't do this. If those men are after you, they're far too close. They'll be watching and they'll catch up to you when you're alone. Here, you're not alone."

Heat from his fingers radiated down into her back and arms and melted the frozen cold she'd felt from the moment he'd told her that she and Maddy'd been found.

"Seth, thank you for offering to help, but Jared Douglas is no one you want to step in front of. He has connections and those connections can get you hurt."

Gently, he turned her to him and then held her biceps as he looked down at her. "Do you think I didn't already figure that out when two guys in military fatigues show up on my doorstep and you don't blink an eye in surprise, you just offer to leave? I meant what I said, Ronnie. I've got my own demons after me. Does it really make sense for you to run when it could be me that they're after? Isn't there safety in numbers?"

She blinked up at him, but it was like all her brain cells had gone numb and she was some little animal just fighting to get free. Fighting to save Maddy, because it was Maddy who would make the ultimate payment. They'd take Maddy away and give her to an abusive man to be raised in a place that was less a home than a prison. Would Seth really help her protect Maddy?

What was it they said? That the eyes were the window to the soul? If she could see Seth's eyes, she might believe him. If she could see his eyes, she might be able to figure out whether to stay or go.

She reached up between them and hesitated, and for the briefest instant, it looked like Seth might pull away. Then he bowed his head, his fine dark head, and she touched his glasses, then lifted them from his temples. A shudder ran though him and his grip tightened painfully on her arms.

Did she really want to do this? Somehow removing his sunglasses felt more intimate than all of the things that she had done as a wife for Jared. There was no going back from this anymore than there had been from her decision to run.

Eyes closed, he lifted his face to her.

Dark, thick lashes made crescents on the pale skin around his eyes. Fine lines from squinting into water and waves etched the sides of his face. Long, aquiline nose like some Roman sculpture. Beautiful. Handsome. Surprised at her audacity, she reached up to stroke the side of his face.

His eyes flashed open and she froze.

Black, as if they were all pupil, the shape rounder than most people's eyes. Black and murky as if his gaze held gold-tinged water and the darkness had consumed any whites. The fairness of his skin made the darkness more intense. Not eyes like any person she'd ever met, at all.

And yet strangely familiar.

It was as if something looked back at her that she could never comprehend: something ancient and lonely and sad. Once more, she thought of unicorns. And the extinction of species.

She shook herself and inhaled as if she'd just come up from deep water.

"So that's what you've been hiding," she said softly. She smiled shyly up at him. "Not so bad."

But reason enough to hide them. Reason enough to live alone. Most people reacted to difference with a cross between pity and revulsion. Seth didn't strike her as the kind of person who would take well to either. But how did this help her to decide whether to stay or go?

"Thank you for trusting me enough to let me see, but I don't think a pair of sunglasses is going to protect Maddy from her father's men." She sighed and turned back to her small athletic bag of belongings.

"So that's what this is? You're trying to save your daughter?"

Ronnie sat down on the edge of the bed and looked at her hands. "My ex would say I've abducted my daughter. He's probably got the courts to agree with him by now. I'd left him and he was fighting for custody. I was fighting back. He was away on a business trip and I told everyone that I was taking Maddy to Disneyworld. We even bought tickets and went to the airport and through security in case he had us watched. We just never got on the plane. Instead we left the airport and I used money I'd saved to buy a small car. We left then and we've been driving ever since—until we came here." She looked up at Seth, who stood silently waiting. "I thought we were safe until I saw Roberta at the dock the other day. She must have recognized me and told Jared. He'll kill me when he finds me. I can't even do the right thing and go to court to get sole custody, because then he'll know where I am."

She felt sick to her stomach and hopeless.

"If he knows where you are already, maybe you can go to court now. Maybe this is the time to stand and fight."

Ronnie shook her head. "Do you know the lawyers he has? I couldn't afford to fight him. Besides, he can show the court how much more he can offer—a big house and servants and everything Maddy could ever want. I can't even put a roof over her head."

He scanned the ceiling. "What's wrong with my roof?"

"It's your roof! I'm—I'm not much better than a kept woman here!"

Seth hauled her up from the bed and into his arms. "You're not a kept woman. Not a kept woman at all. You are a guest in my home until you don't need to be a guest anymore. Do you understand? I—like having you and Maddy here."

His arms tightened around her, sharing his warmth and strength. His broad, hard chest felt wonderful and she could feel the slow steady beat of his heart. His pleasant scent of ocean and cedar filled her senses and she wanted to nestle in and stay here and let all her problems slip away. But she couldn't.

"Sure you do," she said into his chest and tried to push away."Kid's toys underfoot in your pristine living room. Maddy and I nattering at you and destroying your peace. Maddy with all of her questions. You're a bachelor. You don't need this."

"But maybe I do." Said so quietly she had to look up at him to make sure he'd spoken.

Seth nodded. "It can be pretty lonely here at times, especially in winter. I've realized it more since you and Maddy arrived. Sure it's quiet, and I've got Roscoe, but you..." He looked down at her with those fathomless eyes and she felt like she was drowning. And she wanted to drown in those waters. Wanted Seth to know her, to kiss her.

Breathing hard, she tore her gaze away. She was still a married woman, even if she was hiding from her husband. "I'm better than a cat for company, am I? Nice to know."

Seth's rumbling chuckle was a comfort against her. He gentled her hair back over her head, kissed her forehead, and released her. "Stay. Please. Unpack your bag. We'll figure this out together."

He left her to return to the great room and Maddy and she heard their conversation—Maddy's childish chatter and Seth's patient answers. He was astonishingly good with children.

Just like he was good with her? She looked down at her bag and the clothes inside. Do as he suggested? Take a chance?

She'd taken a huge risk leaving Jared, but she realized that trusting someone again felt even more risky. From the living room came the warm rumble of his laughter and she hugged herself, realized she'd liked his arm around her. Realized she missed them, too.

Realized then that she already trusted him too much—and possibly more.

CHAPTER 8

A month later, there'd been no further sign of the men. It had allowed them to slip further into the comfortable rhythm of life together. At times Ronnie couldn't believe her good fortune and had to pinch herself to prove it was real. From her first and second paycheck, she was pretty sure that she had set aside enough money for a first month's rent. Now she just had to save the damage deposit and she and Maddy would have a place of their own.

At the end of yet another sunny day, she stood in the shop overlooking Gibsons Harbor with Carol Dermott, going over the stock orders while Seth took Maddy down to the shore to turn over rocks. Maddy was hanging from one of Seth's arms and he was swinging her around. Maddy's gleeful laughter reached them even in the shop. Where Maddy found this boundless energy, Ronnie couldn't fathom. At the end of each day, it took everything Ronnie had to wash her face and crawl into bed.

"I think your daughter likes Seth," Carol observed as she completed the order form for ten copies of local souvenir calendars. She was a typical new-age, hippy-chick type who had reached her forties with long hair, now gray, contained in a single thick braid down her back. Even on hot days she preferred to wear naturally-dyed, homespun, cinnamon-colored, cotton caftans over leggings. The only thing that changed was the length and color of the legging. Today she wore green ones that barely reached her knees.

She narrowly eyed Ronnie from over her cats-eye glasses and a clutter of bead necklaces. "For that matter, you seem to, too."

Was it question or statement? For a moment Ronnie didn't know what to say. Then she shrugged. "What's not to like? He's helped us immensely, letting us stay at his place until we can get on our feet."

Carol turned and gave her a full-on once over. "Really. As if he takes in stray women and children every day. Or maybe you manage to find a man to protect you everywhere you go."

Not exactly the friendly sort of banter Ronnie was expecting.

"No-o-o. Believe me, that's not it at all." She glanced out the window. Seth and Maddy were crouched down by the water, Maddy concentrating on whatever Seth was showing her. Ronnie sighed. "Men don't usually protect me. At all."

Carol cocked a brow as if she was filing that statement away for future consideration. "Kind of nice to find one that does, I suppose."

"Yes, yes it is." Ronnie realized she was smiling when she looked back at Carol. Over the past weeks they'd been feeling each other out, because apparently Carol Dermott felt a certain level of protectiveness for her boss. "He's a very nice man. A good one."

And one that made her heart beat faster, but she wasn't telling anyone that.

"You like him, maybe even more than your daughter likes him." Carol said as she studied another product catalogue. She looked up and must have caught the shock Ronnie felt.

"Is it that obvious?" she finally said.

Carol nodded and looked away again. "Pretty much. The two of you lean toward each other like trees in the wind. It's like each of you is yearning to touch the other one but doesn't quite dare to do so. I've never seen him like this. He's a kind man, but this is more. Maybe you should rethink this. At least you better be darned sure you know what you're doing before you let this go any further. Understand?"

Ronnie sighed and nodded at the warning. She didn't want to hurt Seth. Besides, being married pretty much played her hand for her, even if she might contemplate more in the still of the night in her bed. She wasn't the kind of woman who gave herself easily to a man. Not anymore.

"He's lucky that he's got you as a friend," Ronnie said.

Carol slung an arm strengthened by years of pottery and working a large weaver's loom around Ronnie's shoulders. "You and Maddy are my friends, too. I've just known Seth a little longer. He's different. Special. And he's been through a lot. He's been wounded deeply—that I can tell."

Ronnie nodded. "Whatever it is, he's not telling."

She caught Carol's surprise.

"He let some hints slip a while back, but he'd not particularly responsive to questions. Mind you, he's all about finding out *my* deepest secrets," Ronnie said with a shake of her head.

"Then you're doing better than me. I've had to parse together cryptic remarks over the past five years.

He doesn't talk about his past at all. Just what has he told you?"

"Not much, but I figure something happened. I think it must have had something to do with his family. A man doesn't get that good with kids by chance." Ronnie nodded through the front window where Seth was hiking up the slope from the water with Maddy thrown over his shoulder like a sack of supplies. Maddy's laughter rang through the glass when he set her down and pushed the door open. Her daughter tumbled in, gave Ronnie a hug, and then turned solemnly to Carol.

"Mrs. Dermott, I 'membered you said that you like snails, so I brought you some." Maddy held up a grubby, seaweed-slimed paw to reveal two small snails, by their greenish color both still very much alive.

Carol went down on one knee to receive her gift. "These are lovely, Maddy. Lovely indeed. Did you know that they're both still alive?"

Maddy nodded. "Mr. Cullen tolded me."

Carol winked up at Ronnie. "These little babies need water to live, honey. How about we take them down to the ocean so that they can be with others like them?"

Her little face screwed up to a frown. "What about if we got a bowl? We could put nice clean tap water in it."

Carol gently shook her head. "That's a different kind of water and these snails would die in it. They need salt, you see."

"If we got water from the ocean?" Maddy asked hopefully.

Ronnie crouched down beside her baby. "Maddy, these little snails need to be in the ocean. You know that, don't you?"

Maddy hung her head and nodded.

"You just wanted Mrs. Dermott to have something nice after all the cookies that she's made you. Is that right?" One meeting with Maddy, and Carol had been bringing fresh chocolate chip oatmeal and organic peanut butter cookies each morning.

Maddy nodded again. "Mr. Cullen has Roscoe... You have me, and I have you, and we both have Mr. Cullen."

Ronnie's heart did a big ka-thunk. Her daughter was worried that Carol was alone.

Carol pulled Maddy into a hug. "Sweetie, I have the biggest, most ferocious kitty at home to keep me company. He might not be Roscoe-big, but he patrols our house like a soldier."

"He does?"

Carol nodded. "Your mom will have to bring you over sometime so you can meet King Ben."

Maddy looked up at Ronnie.

"Of course we can make it happen." Ronnie checked her watch. "And by my watch, Mrs. Dermott should have been out of here fifteen minutes ago, so that she can get home and give King Ben his dinner, isn't that right?"

"It is indeed," Seth said."I'll see you tomorrow, Carol?"

Carol scooped up her purse, gave Maddy a quick hug and a peck on the cheek, then looked from Seth to Ronnie and grinned.

"Wouldn't miss it for the world." Then she cast a serious glance in Ronnie's direction. "You just remember our little conversation."

Then she was gone and Seth cocked his head at Ronnie. "What was that all about?"

Ronnie felt herself color. "Girl stuff, actually. None of your business."

But the way he cocked a brow over his sunglasses, she was pretty sure he knew what girl stuff they'd been talking about.

§

Sitting in the Cherokee on the ride home, Seth couldn't stop himself from glancing over at Ronnie. He'd been doing it far too much today, was too aware of her feminine scent of lilac and the warmth that radiated off her. Actually, she was simply a radiant woman. He'd known it from the first moment he saw her standing at the ferry rail. Would she be spooked if she knew he'd been using his tours to search the coast for her after that one brief glance? Even though his sense of direction had pulled him after her, he'd almost given up hope until he found her in Roberts Creek. And it seemed Carol Dermott had picked up on the chemistry brewing between him and Ronnie—he'd read it plain as day in Carol's knowing glance. There'd been disapproval, too, but Carol would get over it.

He glanced at Ronnie again. Did she know how he felt? Better yet, did she feel it, too? The red-gold strands of her hair had escaped her ponytail and the way they caught the light created a corona around her head.

"What is it?" She met his gaze. "You keep looking at me."

So she'd noticed. Damn. "I was just thinking that it's been a month since the men."

Her slight smile faded, but at least talking about the mysterious spies would change the conversation and would keep things otherwise occupied between them.

"What men, Mommy?"

Ronnie's gaze met his. What would she say?

"Just some men Mr. Cullen saw by the water. They were looking at things," Ronnie explained.

"You mean they were looking for shells like me?" Maddy asked.

Ronnie winced. "Something like that, baby."

"But everything is okay," Maddy asked, a worried little frown on her face.

"Never better, sweetie." Ronnie smiled over her shoulder and Maddy settled back in her car seat again.

After the scare, Seth's enquiries about the men had delivered zero results—the men most likely using a private boat launched from one of the numerous water access points along the coast. Seth and Ronnie had made the decision to continue going about their business, but to also make enquiries about a lawyer for Ronnie. She'd kept an appointment with one only this afternoon, which had allowed them to spend the morning getting kayak rentals and tours out on the water. The entire month, Seth had been loath to leave her—hell, he hadn't wanted to leave her side even when she went in to see the lawyer—but she'd insisted he go. So he'd asked Carol to come in, ostensibly to keep an eye on things, but more so Ronnie and Maddy wouldn't be alone.

"It's good nothing's happened, right?" she said softly and glanced into the back seat where Maddy was talking to her favorite doll. "Maybe the men you saw weren't there about me at all. Maybe they were land speculators looking at the property. Maybe it was all a false alarm."

But the defeated curve of her neck said she didn't believe that at all.

Seth tightened his grip on the steering wheel as they wound along Gower Point Road and then turned off onto the treed driveway to his home. "There are other reasons why those men might be there."

Ronnie shook her head. "So you said. I'd appreciate it if you'd name one."

He could, but he shook his head instead. Ronnie was frightened enough as it was. She didn't need to worry about a danger that hadn't materialized these past five years.

Still... It had taken them five years to find him last time.

"They could have been bird watchers. We do have a pair of bald eagles nesting on the headland. And there's a golden eagle that comes through from time to time. A lot of birders are rabid to get a sighting of a golden."

He felt her doubting blue gaze on him and sighed. "Okay. So not birders."

"Thank you for being honest with me." Surprisingly, she touched the back of his hand as he dropped the car into park. Sparks ran through him from that slightest caress.

He met her gaze though his sunglasses and once more felt the pull of the heart like the instinctual pull of magnetic north. Something had happened when their gazes met that first time. Something he had vowed would never happen again. The first and last time it had happened had brought about a slaughter of his people unlike any seen for countless ages. He had loved Gwyneth O'Connor deeply.

"So how about you and Maddy relax while I make dinner?" Let him get some space between them, because this attraction was becoming too hard to resist. Not with those blue eyes watching him and that pale, smooth skin beckoning. There was no wonder Ronnie's ex-husband wanted her; she was a beautiful woman.

He left Ronnie to organize Maddy and get her into the house while he set to work in the kitchen. Fortunately, Ronnie had parented Maddy into a happy girl who was willing to try most any food and give it a chance. He'd found that beyond tuna sandwiches and hamburgers, she liked salmon and all kinds of vegetables. "Salmon salad it is," he said and set about chopping vegetables.

It was the child's piercing scream that stopped him mid–knife stroke.

CHAPTER 9

It was dead. It was dead. It was dead and its milky, punctured eyes peered up at her like bloody pits, its innards spilled in a bloody mess all over the small pebble beach where Maddy liked to turn over rocks and watch the small crabs scuttle. Ronnie hugged her daughter to her and turned them away from the grisly sight.

"It's okay, Maddy. It's okay." She stroked her distraught daughter's head. "It's dead, all right? Animals die all the time." But not like this. This gray-and-black seal had had its throat cut and its belly sliced open. By the blood on the pebbles, it likely happened right here.

Maddy buried her face in Ronnie's shoulder, her shrieks of horror dying into shuddering sobs. A clatter behind them and then Seth was there, a large kitchen knife in his hand. When he saw the seal, he stopped dead and his face paled.

"Bastards," he mouthed, his expression hard as he scanned the cove.

He knelt down beside the seal and sighed. "It's the old man. He was well known around here, always up and mooching for food from the boaters."

He looked sad as he stroked the dead animal's head. "I thought of him as a friend. I think a lot of people did. He'd follow our kayaks in whenever he caught up to one of the tours. The tourists loved him."

He sighed and stood up. "Why don't you get Maddy up to the house. I'll take care of this."

"But who would do this and why?"

What he thought was masked by those damned glasses of his.

"I think we should leave those discussions for later." He nodded meaningfully at Maddy and she had to agree. She hurried Maddy up the trail to the house and sank down on the couch, cradling her daughter to her.

Maddy snuffled and finally brought her tearful gaze up to Ronnie. "I don't like that he died, Mommy. It hurts right here." She touched her chest. "It hurts to breathe."

"I know, baby. I know." Ronnie rocked Maddy against her. "I feel the same way."

"But you're not crying, Mommy."

"It's because I'm a grown-up, baby. Grown-ups see lots of awful things."

Maddy considered a moment. "I don't want to grow up, then," she said with finality.

"Oh, baby. I wish that were possible and that I could protect you from everything bad forever."

She hugged Maddy to her. God, what if she'd let Maddy go down to the beach alone? She'd been tired enough she'd almost considered it. Why would someone do that to a living creature? Why do it on Seth's beach, leaving the carcass there almost like a calling card for someone to find?

Unless... she stiffened. Would Jared's men do such a cruel thing? Surely to goodness Jared wouldn't. They'd never had pets, but he'd always patted the neighbor's dog and he'd enjoyed seeing wildlife when they were young enough to go camping together. But since Maddy was born, Jared had changed—at least toward her. Could he give the order to do something so heartless?

She shivered.

"Mommy?"

"Yes, baby?" Ronnie stroked Maddy's back.

"Are you scared? 'Cause I am."

"Nothing's going to hurt you, baby. I won't let anything hurt you, okay?" She cuddled Maddy on her lap until the small shudders ceased and gradually Maddy's breathing slowed into the steady rhythm of sleep. Gently she carried her daughter back to her bedroom, where sunlight through blinds slatted the bed. Ronnie tucked Maddy in, then sat beside her, stroking her soft skin, her hair, inhaling her scent of innocence. She was so young, so vulnerable, and should never experience anything like today's shock.

Nothing like this would ever happen again and nothing would ever harm Maddy worse. Nothing at all. Ronnie would give her life to make sure of it.

But the Sunshine Coast was beginning to feel less than safe.

From the great room came the sound of Seth returning. There were clanks and bangs from the kitchen and then silence until the sound of Seth's shower running came from the other side of the house. When the water stopped she finally left Maddy sleeping and went out to the kitchen. He leaned over the kitchen sink, peering out the sun-filled window with his back to her. His khaki shirt was damp at the shoulders, his dark hair slick and wet around his ears. Anger stiffened the slope of his shoulders and positively radiated from him. This wasn't someone you wanted angry at you. Thank God Seth was on their side.

She hesitated a moment, but then crossed to him to lay a hand on his arm. "I'm so sorry. I know you care about the animals."

She looked up at him and was too aware of the furious heat radiating from him. Just this once he hadn't replaced his sunglasses and his opaque amber eyes were deep wells of sorrow when he looked down at her. Where did he get such eyes? How did the world look to him when he seemed to look into her? She had so many questions, but a tingle of need ran through her like an echo to the need she saw rise like a dolphin in his gaze.

"You were right," he said, his voice gruff and deep. He shook off her touch and turned back to the window. "You should leave."

It felt like he'd struck her, just as Jared had struck her. She staggered back, trying to figure out what she'd done. Her history with Jared had shown her that it was always her fault. Always.

"What? Why? Is it because..."

He glanced at her as if just the sight of her pained him. "I don't need the trouble you bring."

It made so much sense given her past experiences. All his protestations about being there for her and

Maddy weren't worth the breath he used to say them. Promises, like to love and protect all the days of your life, were really just meant to be broken. But she'd never break her promise to Maddy. That was different. That was blood. That was soul deep.

And yet...and yet Seth had said that there was another possible reason the men might have come—something that haunted his past. Was this his attempt to protect her from whatever it was that might have come for him?

For Maddy, she should listen to him.

She sucked in a breath and nodded. "I'm sorry the seal was killed. It's horrible. I'm sorry Maddy and I disturbed your life, if that's what the problem is. But if this is about you, then I'm going to say what you said to me—aren't you better off with other people here?"

Seth stayed silent at the window. There was nothing more she could do.

"All right. Just let me get my things packed and I'll wake Maddy and we'll go."

She checked her watch. "If I get going, I just might make the next ferry."

She turned and left the room, hearing Seth stir behind her. He was likely relieved that she'd made it so easy.

§

From the kitchen Seth heard Ronnie shifting around her and Maddy's rooms. There the quiet slide of dresser drawers. There the smooth rumble of a sliding closet door. The soft pad of feet. In truth his sensitive hearing had allowed him to constantly track her movements since she'd come into his home. Ronnie's presence had been a comfort, a sense that perhaps he was slowly coming back to life. She made him smile. She made him feel alive and protective and—and, damnation, loving! And Maddy was the crowning jewel. She brought joy.

Once he'd had a young son, but Caleb had died in the slaughter.

He filled a glass from the faucet and drank it down to steady himself. He was doing the right thing. He peered out over the kitchen window herb pots to the forest beyond. His house that had always felt snug and safe now felt as laid open as a sea turtle turned on its back. Something hung over it, ready to gut it. Were they out there even now, watching the house from the trees? Please let them wait long enough that Ronnie and Maddy could get free.

Because Ronnie's guess had been terribly, horribly right. The dead old man on the beach hadn't been a message for her; it had been for him. His seal kin slaughtered just as his old enemies had slaughtered his kind so long ago in Ireland. But at least Ronnie's fear had meant that he hadn't had to expose the real reason they were all in danger. This way she could leave safely.

She came into the kitchen with two packed bags in her hands and Maddy's stuffed animals under her arms. "I'll just get these to the car and get Maddy."

By the shadows under her eyes, she'd been crying and Seth winced and nodded. Damnation, he didn't want them to leave. He loved Maddy's laughter and Ronnie's gentle guidance of her daughter. She'd been the same to him—gentle, giving, and yet strong enough to rise to the occasion to protect her baby and herself.

Resignedly she moved past him to the main door of the house and he went after her to the doorway to make sure that nothing happened to her in her foray outside to the driveway and her old Civic. Silently, she loaded the suitcases in the back and put the toys where Maddy could access them in the backseat. Already the property felt empty, the laughter and life drained out of it. He groaned.

Dear God, what was he doing? How, in such a short time, could he believe that he loved her? Why did he feel like simply baring his chest to the predators just to get it over with?

When she turned back to him and the house, there was a funereal slope to her shoulders as if she had accepted that her life was over. Her ex-husband's men were snapping at her heels and it was almost a certainty that she wouldn't elude them.

Was that what he'd done to her? Sent her off into an unsafe world with the belief that a guillotine hung over her head? He knew what it was like to live like that. He couldn't be that cruel. At the least she deserved to know that it wasn't her situation, but his, that forced her to leave. That there was nothing out there pursuing her.

Head down, she went past him into the house and he caught her scent of lilac. She crossed the great room for the kitchen and her rooms.

"Ronnie."

She stopped at the entrance to the short hallway.

"I need to explain."

"No. You don't." She shook her head, but didn't look at him. "I understand completely. It's one thing to take some destitute woman and her child into your home. It's another thing entirely when said woman and child draw danger to your home. It could be Roscoe or you next if we stay, and that's not fair to you. Now it's better if we get on our way."

She headed down the hall to Maddy's room, but he was across the great room and snagged her arm before she could enter. He hauled her, protesting, back into the kitchen and forced her down into a chair. Then he knelt in front of her.

"Listen to me. I have something to tell you."

Her startled gaze firmed on him, waiting. Good. She *was* listening.

"The old man's death wasn't about you. It was about me. There are people out there who've been searching for me. Now, apparently, they've found me and they want to send me running. Killing the old man was an attempt to spook me and send me off on my own."

She blinked. "Why? Why would someone want to do that?"

What could he tell her? She'd seen his eyes and knew he was different, but there was too good a chance she'd be repulsed by what he was. Whatever happened, he didn't want her to hate him.

He sighed and looked at his hands. Hands that had failed another woman and child so many years before. Ronnie deserved to know.

"Years ago my people, my clan, were deemed to be—heretics—in the eyes of the church. We were hunted down and destroyed and so we lived solitary lives. Since those horrible days, the church grew and changed and as a result, some of us came together and risked forming a community. I was one of them. I fell in love with a woman in another town who had been betrothed to a man she didn't love. We were married. We had a son. But unbeknownst to us, a small faction of the church continued to hunt my people. My wife's ex-fiancée exposed us and the faction found us. And killed us. My wife and child died in my arms. Everyone I knew, as well. So many innocents. I think I was the only one to escape. But the men saw me leave and they and their kind have pursued me ever since, over the years."

He waited to hear what she'd say. Her eyes shifted color as if each fleeting thought was a wave on the sea. Grief. Worry. Anger. Pity, and back to sorrow. Her hand rose to touch his cheek.

"What you've lived through. My God, Seth. The horrors you've seen. You could have told me that you're a refugee."

Her touch was like the lightest breeze, or a silken scarf sinking through water, but it conveyed a warmth that reached him through the years of cold. He should pull away, but her concern brought him deeper into her touch.

"What I'm trying to say is that you don't have to worry. Your ex-husband hasn't found you. The faction has found me. You're safe if you leave me to my battles. In fact, it's better that way." Better because he could not bond any farther, though every part of his being wanted to do so. This instant attraction was what he'd felt with Gwyneth so long ago and hadn't felt once in the years between.

Ronnie's fingers spread and became her smooth palm against his cheek. He should pull away. He should help her carry her daughter from the house and send them away to the safety of their lives.

Instead he caught her wrist and kissed her palm. She shivered and bowed her head, then leaned in to rest her head on his shoulder.

"I have to keep Maddy safe, but I can't leave you alone to face this." Her voice was the barest of whispers, but he could feel her breath through the light cotton of his shirt.

His hands stroked her hair and slid down over her shoulders to her back and waist. Gently, he set her away from him. Her hair was a curtain around her face. "You have to. Truly. For Maddy. These men are ruthless. You saw their work on the beach."

Another visible shiver and then she brought her head up to look at him. "That's why I can't leave you. I have to know you're both safe."

The way she looked at him, he couldn't look away. He was lost in her eyes the way he'd been lost at sea back so long ago. But where he'd once been looking for a way to end his life, Ronnie was a way back to life itself.

She leaned in toward him and he met her halfway. Soft lips parted before his. Warm mouth, at first tentative, but then matching his hunger, and he was famished and ravenous. His hands caught her fair hair and held her in place until her smaller hands suddenly pushed on his chest.

Seth pulled back and Ronnie looked up at him. Tears flowed down her cheeks as she caressed his cheek. "I'm sorry. I can't. I'm still married, Seth. I'm not giving Jared anymore ammunition against me than he has."

He knew she was right, but by all the waves in the sea, he wanted her—to have, to hold, to protect, to cherish. But his desires were unfair to her. Why would a woman wish to be with a man who was cursed to only stay with her for a year and a day? After that he was doomed to return to the sea. It was the curse of the selkie who fell in love with a human. Something she could never know.

"Then perhaps it is better if you and Maddy go. You can find a new life that doesn't put you in danger and I will fight my battle and win or lose as the fates decree."

She sat back from him, apparently studying his face. Then she sighed again and slung her arms around his neck and leaned in until he could feel her breath on his face. "Help me find a safe place for Maddy until this is over. Apparently I can't leave you like this. There's two of them and only one of you. I've fought for what I wanted before. Apparently, what I want now is you."

Then she kissed him again. Hard.

§

What the hell am I doing? a part of Ronnie screamed. Maybe it was her better judgment, but this was the same voice that had told her she should stick it out with Jared so that Maddy could have a family. Sitting in the flooding sunshine with Seth before her, she knew the voice was wrong again. Seth was a good man, the first in her life since her father died when she was seven. He didn't deserve to die like that seal had. Nothing living did. She was doing the right thing by staying.

She inhaled his musk of brine and cedar and her desire for him burned hotter.

Are you sure it's not only the lust that's keeping you here? Think of Maddy. Think of her safety.

"How can I make sure Maddy's safe? I can't have her in danger while we settle things. But—today I signed the papers to start legal proceedings against Jared. It's done and Jared's going to know where I am. The lawyer arranged to get me on the docket for an emergency hearing tomorrow. I just have to pray things go my way. I can't keep running and hiding. It just makes it worse when you're found."

She looked around Seth's beautiful house and thought of the destruction he had seen. Funny, she didn't remember reading anything about the massacre of a village, but then horrors happened everyday in this world and the news channels didn't broadcast everything. But it explained the hint of accent she'd heard in Seth's voice, though it was so faint it was as if he'd had a great deal of time to lose it. She wondered where he was from originally and all that he had left behind.

The high-beamed ceilings, the low-slung couch, and the huge stone fireplace of the great room gleamed in the sunlight. Outside, the stone patio and the trail led down to the turquoise waters of the cove.

"Not facing the danger just means you have so much more to lose when it finally finds you."

Seth's throat worked. "Like you and Maddy."

Leaning into him again was like coming home. His arms around her gave her strength for what was to come. "We can do this, Seth. We can fight them off."

His breath was warm on her head where he kissed her hair. "At least this time we know they're coming."

CHAPTER 10

The next day bloomed as beautiful as almost every day on the Sunshine Coast—at least since Ronnie had arrived. The sun rose languorously, filling the sky first with apricot that topped the waves with red amber. Then the sun's rays burst like a crown above the eastern arm of Seth's cove and the sky turned gold, pink, and blue as the day rolled over the sky as regular and constant as the tide.

Dressed in her best blue dress and green silk scarf for the court hearing, she stood in the kitchen hoping the sun's glare off the windows hid her presence. She sipped a newly brewed latte and looking out at the deep blue, peaceful ocean. Hard to believe, with the soft breeze whispering in the trees, that yesterday the beach had been a scene of savagery such as only a human can wreak upon the weaker species.

And its own kind.

She knew all about *that* first-hand.

She shivered and the coffee spilled warm over her fingers and into the sink. She licked her fingers and listened to Maddy hum to her doll as she ate her breakfast of Coast Muesli, warm milk, and fresh organic peaches. Today would be the start of a new life. No more fear. No more running.

A warmth in the air warned her of Seth's presence though he made no sound as he came up behind her.

"You shouldn't stand so close to the window. You're far too exposed," he said and lightly caught her shoulder to guide her back into the kitchen. His dark hair was slicked back from his shower, but his forelock still fell, untamed, over his now unshielded eyes. They were dark and intense as a storm over the ocean—or the ocean's depths—and again she felt like he could look right through her and know her as no other man ever had. This morning he'd traded in his usual faded t-shirt and shorts for a pair of navy chinos and a polo shirt.

"I was just enjoying the morning. It's so peaceful here—or it was." She glanced back toward the cove, then turned back and assessed his clothing. "So what's the occasion?"

He looked down at himself, then checked out the simple blue jersey shift she wore that skimmed her athletic figure. "I thought we were going to court."

"I thought *I* was. It might give them the wrong idea if you come in with me. And first we have to drop Maddy off with Carol. Thank goodness she can take care of Maddy for a few days."

Seth nodded, looking grave. "Let's hope it's all over that quickly. You look nice, by the way. The green scarf sets off your hair."

They joined Maddy at the table and she looked up at Seth. Her eyes widened. She set down her spoon. "What happened to your eyes?" she asked guilelessly. "They look strange."

Seth shook his head and glanced at Ronnie. "Nothing happened, actually. I was born this way, Maddy."

She mulled that over for a moment. "Do they hurt? Do things look different?"

Seth bent down and looked Maddy eye-to-eye. "Well, I can't rightly say, can I? This is the only way I've ever seen things, but right now I see a little blonde-haired girl who has her breakfast to finish." He tapped his finger on Maddy's nose and she giggled and kept on eating, but she kept throwing little glances in Seth's direction as if she was figuring something out.

Seth and Ronnie ate a quick breakfast of cereal and fresh blueberries, then packed everyone into the Cherokee and headed for town. Seth wore his sunglasses again.

Carol was waiting when they arrived at her house in the woods. It was a low-slung little place tucked up against a side hill, with gray shingle siding and a steeply slanted roof that made Ronnie think of elves—except for the awkward-looking, two-story tower built at one end. The architectural monstrosity even had a small porch like a widow's walk around the top story.

Carol opened her front door as they crunched up the gravel driveway and she welcomed Maddy with open arms. "Welcome to my home, sweet thing. I have gardening for us to do and adventures in the woods and maybe you can help me weave a nice pot holder for your mom."

Carol looked up at Ronnie, but then looked away.

"That sounds fun!" Maddy said, checking with Ronnie. "Can I meet King Ben now?"

Ronnie rolled her eyes. "Some things are priorities, don'cha know."

Carol nodded toward the open door. "Come on in, then. Let's get the obligatories over with."

The house was dark, its low eaves and small windows allowing in only limited light. Not what Ronnie'd expected at all. Not with Carol's pottery and weaving. She couldn't imagine doing either without better lighting. To the left of the entry stood a dimly-lit living room that held a fireplace, a television, and a worn couch with a dark green slipcover that had been worn shiny. It was a lonely looking room. On the other side of the entry, a door closed off what might be an office. Smells of coffee and cigarette smoke from the hallway toward the rear of the house said that the kitchen lay that way.

Ronnie stopped. She hadn't known that Carol smoked. She looked up at Seth and his nostrils flared as if he noticed something, too.

"Have you got company?" he asked.

"Just you! So what's got you two needing a babysitter for Maddy?" Carol asked as she turned into another hallway that ran toward the house's tower. "It seems rather sudden."

She glanced back at Ronnie and for a moment Ronnie thought she saw something hard and unyielding. Then it was gone as Carol slanted a brow at her in question. "Is this because of yesterday?"

Yesterday. So much had happened. But she was pretty sure Carol referred to their conversation. Ronnie shook her head.

"Not really. Some things have come up—like I have a court date for me to deal with a family matter."

"Really." Carol blinked as if she didn't know quite what to believe. "I guess that's good, then."

With no further comments, she led them to a small doorway that Seth had to duck through. The door itself was made of stout wood. Beyond it, a square room was filled with bookshelves on all four solid walls with a single reading chair in the space. A wrought iron spiral stair cut up through the center of the tower to what Ronny assumed was a similar room up above.

"King Ben likes to lie in the sunlight on the couch I have up there," Carol said and waved Maddy on ahead of her.

Maddy scooted up the stairs and then put her head through the rail to peer down at Ronnie. "Come on, Mommy! This is fun. You should see!" She pulled her head back through the cast iron railing and her footfall clattered up the rest of the stairs. "Oh! He's so big!" Her voice floated down to them.

"We better go rescue King Ben from the ministrations of my daughter." Ronnie started up the stairs with Seth at her heels.

They were halfway up, listening to Maddy's crooning to the cat, when the click of the door sounded behind them.

As one, Ronnie and Seth turned. The wooden door was closed and Carol was gone. As they stood there, the room filled with the sound of a key turning.

§

"What the hell!" Seth looked from Ronnie's startled face to the empty room below. He bounded down the stairs for the door. Locked. "Carol! What the be-jeezus's going on?"

He knew she was there. He could hear her breathing as if she leaned against the door.

"Open the door, Carol. Tell me to my face what's going on."

"You know what's happening, Seth. It's over for you and your kind. You weren't a problem as long as you were alone, but when you bring a woman into things—well, we can't have that now, can we?"

Stunned, he didn't know what to say. Somehow Carol knew what he was. She knew what Ronnie meant to him—or was growing to mean. Betrayal cut deeply into his breast. "I thought you were my friend."

Silence a moment. "I thought I was, too. But then I realized what was happening. I'd been set here to keep track of you when you first came. You've never been far ahead of them, Seth. They could have killed you any time. But it's one thing to let some soulless beast live out its life. It's another thing entirely to have it breeding."

"Seth? What's she talking about? Why are we locked in?" Ronnie stood behind him. She'd heard what was said.

He closed his eyes for strength but it wasn't there. He turned to Ronnie and caught her hands. "I haven't been completely honest with you."

She eased her hands free. "I sort of figured. Soulless beast? What does that mean?" Her gaze was a sea of confusion.

"Ronnie, it's not the way it sounds." He took a step toward her, but she held up a warning hand at the same time as her eyes brimmed with tears.

"Seth, you know how I feel about you, but tell me what she means before you come any closer. Carol tried to warn me off. What was she trying to warn me about?"

Clearly she was torn between her concern for her daughter and her desire to believe in him. Damnation, there was no way he could lie through this one, but... "Everything I've told you is the truth."

Her hands flexed into fists at her sides and her expression went bleak. He was losing her by hiding the truth.

"Then what haven't you told me?" she asked.

Her eyes smoldered with a ferocious strength he wouldn't have thought she had. She wasn't afraid of him—not for herself at any rate.

"I—told you everything I could. Everything that I dared."

"Really." She crossed her arms. "So just how does some poor slob who lost his whole community—who let me think he was a refugee—come to be called a soulless beast by a woman he thought was his friend?"

Who was he kidding? It was over. All the years of thinking he was hiding. Of thinking he was free. It had all been a sham and the enemy hadn't lost him—they'd just thought he wasn't worth doing anything about. Until Ronnie. He might as well tell her.

He slumped in the room's chair and closed his eyes.

"Mommy? Are you going to come up and see King Ben? He's really nice. He's purring."

Seth opened his eyes and read Ronnie's indecision. Fatigue and failure ate away his resolve. Always a coward. So long ago, if he hadn't lured away someone else's intended, if he'd been home instead of being barred from his family by the selkie curse, if he had been quicker and stealthier when he came to shore, perhaps he wouldn't have been shot. And perhaps he wouldn't have passed out and would have been able to help Gwyneth and Caleb escape. Instead, they met the knife.

"Go be with your daughter. I promise that I'll stay down here and not be a problem. They'll likely be here for me soon."

He sank back in the chair, but there was no sound of feet on stairs. Only the fragrance of her rose shampoo and her soft breathing as if she was still undecided. Well he *had* decided.

"I'm a soulless beast, remember? You don't want or need any part of me and I don't want any part of you." He slumped back in the chair and finally footfalls receded up the stairs. Soft voices came from up above. Maddy's childish delight and Ronnie's calming influence with an undertone of grief. At least they were together.

Now he just had to do whatever it took to keep them safe.

CHAPTER 11

Carol's turret was clearly her work room, so in that, at least, she hadn't lied. The space was sunny, about twelve feet by twelve feet with extradeep windows on all four sides so the space was filled with light. A full-sized loom filled the middle of the room, with cubbies holding rainbows of different colored wool on the remaining walls between the windows and ranks of small drawers below like apothecary's cupboards. A couch and coffee table were set up facing southwestward where the Georgia Strait and Howe Sound gleamed blue in the morning. On the couch was spread a blue hand-woven throw, and sprawled on the throw was, indeed, the king of cats.

King Ben was golden as a tiger's pelt but instead of stripes he had perfect round rosettes of black, and raccoon rings that went around his tail. Regardless of the tenseness of her situation, King Ben had assumed that loose-limbed sprawl that only cats can accomplish. And he was purring, a comforting deep rumble that filled the space as if to say that all was going to be well, when clearly it wasn't.

Maddy perched on the couch beside the cat and gently stroked his back. The tip of his tail flicked like a whisk and his ears wavered between Maddy and Ronnie's position so though he might look relaxed, he was perfectly aware that something was wrong. Unlike her daughter.

Ronnie scanned the room for a weapon, but there were no knives or scissors lying about. She started on the drawers, searching their contents one by one. More yarn. Darning needles. Knitting needles—she kept out the longest metal ones. Under more wool, another drawer gave up a steel seam ripper, like small pointy sheers the length of her palm. She tested them against her finger and drew blood. Clearly these sharp little sheers were not what Carol had intended her to find. She stuffed them in her blue shift's pocket and draped her scarf to hide the bulge against future need and kept on searching, but her initial assessment still stood. Carol had removed all the weapons. The seam ripper and the needles she'd probably either overlooked or she'd underestimated their potential.

Ronnie edged over to the stairwell to peer down. A pair of brown leather shoes attached to navy chino-clad legs, so Seth hadn't moved.

She edged back and sank down on the coffee table across from Maddy.

Maddy looked up at her. "Can we get a kitty like this someday? I think he and Roscoe would like to play together. Don't you? They could be best friends just like you and Mr. Cullen."

Best friends. For a space brief in time, she'd thought it might happen. "I'm afraid that probably isn't going to happen, but someday we might get a kitten. In fact, I'm sure of it. We'll get a kitten as soon as we have our own place. Will that do?"

Maddy frowned. "You mean we aren't going to stay with Mr. Cullen anymore? But what about Roscoe and Mr. Cullen? I thought we liked them."

Oh, God, this was what happened when you dragged children into fledgling relationships—they were left disappointed when things didn't work out. She should have known better on so many fronts. She hugged Maddy to her to comfort them both.

From below came the sound of the turret door opening, a shout, and the crashing sound of a battle.

§

He'd heard them coming no matter that they used stealth to try to catch him by surprise. His preternatural hearing was good for underwater, but it also worked well in these situations. Like eavesdropping on Ronnie and her daughter. At least maybe now he could keep them safe, convince Carol and her bosses that Ronnie really wasn't involved. At least they must know that Maddy wasn't his daughter!

By all the gods and goddesses over the ages, he had to make sure they understood!

He'd stood to one side of the door, his heart pounding, the windowless room ticking around him, the scent of the books filling the shelves heavy in the air as if all the words had weight. Then came the soft click of the lock tumblers falling. A heartbeat pause.

The door slammed open and five men flooded in, clad in camo fatigues and jackets.

There was a chance that his superior strength could ram right through them and on to freedom, but he wasn't leaving Ronnie and Maddy to feel their wrath. He punched one man in the face and felt cheekbones give. Kicked out at another and caught him in the gut. But five to one were never good odds in a brawl. As soon as he fought one off, another jumped on his back. He backed toward the wall, but it was too late. Maddy's shriek came from upstairs and the sound of a struggle. One of the men had got past to the stairs.

He stopped fighting and held his hands up facing his enemies. Three were young, brawny, crewcut men with zealot's fire in their eyes. The fourth was older with scars across his cheek, but with the same facial bone structure as a harsh fisherman, Jacob Ryan, who had lost his fiancée to a gentler man who came from the sea. Jacob had been a deeply religious man. This man, like his ancestor, wore hate like an extra layer of skin as he clutched his gun. He reeked of church incense, as well. Just like his ancestor. By his expression, he'd take pleasure in the weapon's use. The kind of man who could butcher the old man and not blink. His gaze held a gleam of malice and triumph as if racial memory told him he faced an old foe. But then, perhaps Jacob Ryan had made sure that his offspring knew that they had a score to settle against something unholy. Sometime in history, Jacob Ryan's family and the church had joined forces.

At the top of the stairs, the fourth young man shoved Ronnie before him with Maddy in her arms.

"Listen. They have nothing to do with this. They're just strangers who needed a hand so I offered them a place to stay."

Ryan hooked his head at the man up the stairs. The young man shoved Ronnie and Maddy down ahead of him.

"Did you hear me? They aren't like me. They're innocents."

Ryan's dead eyes just looked at him. "Innocents don't fall in love with something soulless." He nodded at his men and they lunged for Seth, pinioning his arms against the bookshelves. He fought them off, but scar face lunged. Something sharp bit the side of Seth's neck and he froze. What had they done?

He had time to look to Ronnie—she was screaming at the men.

Then the room faded out and his legs gave.

It was the throb of an engine and the slap of water that woke him. That and the softness of something warm pressed in front of him. He lay on his side and tried to shift position, but ropes trussed his hands behind his back and his bent legs, and every part of his body protested. He opened his eyes, but there was only throbbing darkness—and the sound of too-fast breathing. The scent of faint roses and fear filled the diesel-tanged air.

"Ronnie?" he whispered. His voice was hoarse and his mouth tasted like fifteen years of tidal mud. His head pounded with whatever they had given him and lethargy ate his will to move.

"Here," whispered softly. "I've got Maddy. She's finally cried herself to sleep." The warmth and softness stirred against him. "They've got us stashed in some sort of locker on a fishing boat. Are you okay? They gave you a beating when you went down."

That explained the pain that came from everywhere, not that he hadn't felt worse. "Are you and Maddy okay? Did they hurt you?"

"N-no." But he felt her tremble against him. "Just... Maddy's terrified. So am I. What are they going to do to us, Seth?"

It was pretty clear that it was nothing good. "Let's just wait and see, all right? I'll get us out of here somehow."

But he needed a plan. What the hell could he do, trapped like a humpback whale in nets? There was no place to go but down—dragging Ronnie and Maddy with him. He couldn't let that happen.

He pulled against his bonds, but whoever tied his limbs was an expert. They didn't budge—which meant that they were pretty much at the mercy of their captors.

"Seth?" Ronnie's voice.

"Hmm?"

"I'm sorry I reacted like I did. I don't think you're a soulless beast, no matter what Carol Dermott says. I heard you trying to bargain for our safety. Thank you."

A small, damp warmth found his shoulder where she kissed him.

He sighed. "You had every right to react like you did. Maybe Carol was telling the truth. You don't know me—or my kind. How can you be expected to trust someone who's not even human?"

He heard the catch in her breath just as something rattled above them and the lid of the locker swung open into the too-bright daylight of late evening.

Four men reached in and dragged Maddy out of Ronnie's arms. Maddy woke, screaming, and Ronnie launched herself out of the locker. Seth struggled to sitting, but the muzzle of a gun stopped him. Ronnie gathered a struggling Maddy to her and held on tight.

"You can't have my baby." She was ferocious and beautiful in the sunlight, facing off against the circle of four men.

"Fine by us, love," said Ryan's descendant, exiting from the wheelhouse cabin.

They were on a salmon trawler, but its huge fishing spars didn't run any lines. The deck pitched under them, from three-foot waves that stretched out from the boat in every direction, but the coastal mountains hung to the east and Vancouver Island was still to the west. So they were still in Georgia Straight at least, and by the look of the coastline, a good ways north of Howe Sound. A lot of traffic ran through here during the day, but now the sun was sinking. The day-trippers and sailboats would be heading back for harbor, leaving only the Alaskan cruise ships, the coastal cargo ships, and the heavy tugs hauling their barges up and down the main channel. But the main channel was west of where they were. Were their captors planning on throwing them overboard? He wouldn't put it past them.

The westering sun hung low over the Vancouver Island Mountains, painting the sky brilliant fuchsia and orange. The waves turned umber and black and Ryan's descendant nodded to his men. One of them went to the rear of the fishing boat and hauled on a line. Something clunked against the hull as two other men herded Ronnie and Maddy to the gunnels.

"What are you doing? You let them go!" Disregarding the gun in his face, Seth struggled to his feet. The roll of the boat almost pitched him to the deck.

"Your wish is my command." Ryan turned back to the men. "Get the girl in first."

What the hell was going on? Two of the men fought Maddy out of Ronnie's arms. Seth threw himself out of the locker, but his tied feet and arms betrayed him and he sprawled on the deck, managed to get his knees under him in time to see Maddy lowered kicking and screaming over the side of the boat. Then two of the men shoved Ronnie over the side.

Seth fought to his feet and threw himself over the side, to a blast of gunfire. Something burned his side as he slammed into black water.

Cold. Cold enough to snap a human's mouth open in shock so that water could flood in.

But he wasn't human. He clamped his mouth closed and dolphin-kicked toward daylight and one pair of kicking legs. Beyond, the large hull of the fishing boat left them and churned away southward, but beside Ronnie was a long, slim hull that sat high in the water. Kayak.

He surfaced beside Ronnie, but struggled to stay afloat. Breath came hard. Pain filled his side and he knew what that meant. But Ronnie caught his polo-shirt and held him up with one hand while her other white-knuckled the cockpit of a double kayak. One of his.

Maddy. Where was Maddy?

Then he spotted her pale curls in the front cockpit of the big kayak. That, at least, was a relief.

"They didn't give us any paddles," Ronnie said through chattering teeth.

Ten minutes in this water was about all anyone could last without hypothermia setting in. "You have to get in the kayak. That's the only way you're going to survive."

She shook her head. "I'm not leaving you tied up in the water. You'll drown."

Then her face brightened. "Hold on a minute. I think I've got something."

She let go of the kayak and Maddy screamed as her mother went under. Then cold fingers worked at his wrists and gradually the rope parted until he jerked his hands free. He grabbed Ronnie and half threw her up the side of the kayak.

"Get in. I'm more equipped for the water than you."

She handed back a tiny set of metal sheers. "Here. For your legs."

She'd hauled her torso up over the cockpit and swung a leg over the back of the kayak by the time he was free. Then she slid into the rear cockpit to sit drenched and shivering in her sodden blue dress, her green scarf a tangle around her neck. The evening wind was cool over the increasingly rough waves. To the northwest, heavy clouds blocked most of the sunset. The winds caught the kayak and it floundered through the water.

She pulled a cord on the fiberglass kayak hull and from the rear came the thunk of the rudder falling into place. Then she shook her head. "This isn't going to work. These boats are stable when you've got paddles, but without them, even with the rudder, the wind will just catch the boat and our bodies and blow us sideways. We're prime to capsize. I need to stay in the water to keep it pointed into the wind."

Seth reached up and grabbed her hand. "You listen to me. You're not thinking straight. You come back in this water and you'll die for sure. Understand?"

Her blue eyes found his and gradually the reason returned. She nodded.

"Okay. Now I'm going to leave you and swim to shore. When I get there I'll bring help and get you out of here. Okay?"

She looked down at him, uncertain. Then her gaze firmed on his chest. "Are you bleeding? You are!" She leaned down for him and the kayak tipped perilously.

"It's nothing. Just a flesh wound. They caught me when I went over the side." But now that he paid attention, it felt like something more. Bones grated in his side as if the bullet's impact had broken something.

He pulled away from her. "Remember what I said. I'll be back for you. Now you focus on keeping Maddy and you safe. Okay?"

"Seth, that's an impossible swim. No one can make it that far." Then she did the strangest thing—she unwrapped her scarf from her neck and handed it to him. "For your wound," she said

He grinned up at her, warmed by her concern and tied the scarf around his chest. "But I'm a soulless beast, remember?"

He ducked his head under and swam.

CHAPTER 12

The midsummer night wind was freezing as Seth stumbled to shore in his cove after the long, painful swim. The wound in his side was worse than he'd let on—even though he'd bound it with Ronnie's scarf. The injury had slowed him down, though even in human form he was a powerful swimmer. It was a long time since he'd swum so far as a human and he wasn't finished his efforts for the night.

He staggered to his feet, the stars cold and distant overhead, and wavered up the gravel beach to the house. There were things he needed if this was to work. Inside he filled a watertight bag, ate a granola bar for energy, and made a 9-1-1 call to the Coast Guard Search and Rescue before digging out papers, placing them in a dry bag that could be worn on a lanyard around the neck, and returning to the beach. There, he searched amongst the boulders on the shore. His skin. He'd been swimming as a seal when he had first caught Ronnie's scent. He'd transformed to catch sight of her, but had changed back when too many people peered off the ferry. He kept his skin hidden here, against his enemies finding him. He'd hidden it in a place he could access easily, because this was the natural part of him.

The part of him Ronnie could never know. And now she would if he was going to save her.

To save her, he would have to lose her.

He struggled to shift the boulder aside and revealed a stout orange pelican box. He snapped it open to reveal a silken hide of black and silver. Him. Coming home again. He stroked the soft fur and his skin trembled. His flesh vibrated in anticipation of change. When he hauled out the fur and flung it open around his shoulders, the voice of the sea called to him. Once he had thought that was all he should hear. He would just keep on swimming until he could swim no more and lose himself in the animal.

But the animal had too much common sense. It was that which had saved him from his foolhardy plunge after he'd lost everything.

"Help me now, please!" he sent a prayer to ancient Celtic gods and released his hold on his human form.

Arms and legs reduced to flippers. Fur adhered to flesh. Bones softened and his ears sank away until he was a sleek-sided bull seal, amongst the rocks of the cove. With his powerful tail, he knocked the boulder back over his hiding place, placed his head through the loop on the drybag he'd filled, and surged over the stone and into the water. A flick of his flippers and he was racing through waves, away from the land, out into dark water.

§

Night crept over the eastern horizon as Ronnie fought her fears and tried to calm her frightened daughter. Color seeped from the sky turning bright blue to dust, then dark gray, then a darkening indigo the color of the space between stars. The cold wind cut through Ronnie's sodden clothes. At least Maddy didn't have to contend with that—except where the waves caught her. Of course there weren't any spray skirts on the kayak, so any wave that hit them broadside inexorably filled the cockpits with water. The kayak's sizeable cargo holds might keep it afloat, but they did nothing to keep the paddlers from death by hypothermia. Maddy was wearing only t-shirt and shorts. Ronnie's own blue dress clung to her skin.

"Honey, I want you to scooch down as low as you can in the cockpit. It you can get right under the transom, even better. Okay? That will keep you out of the wind and give you a little shelter."

She waited for a reply.

"Maddy? You answer me this minute!"

The command worked, for a small voice got caught and torn away by the wind. Maddy twisted around to look at her mother, her face a pale smear in the darkness.

Oh, God, she needed to save her daughter. Children succumbed to hypothermia more easily. If they were together, they could share their warmth. It might be the last thing Ronnie had to give. But even the movement of Maddy's small frame provided a sail for the wind to catch. The kayak swung sideways into the wind and the waves caught it.

Ronnie barely had time to shift her weight against the kayak's desire to roll.

"Maddy, you get down in the cockpit like I said, and I want you to pull your knees up to your chest and hold onto them. Do you hear me?"

Maddy gave a listless nod, but her little head disappeared into the depths of the cockpit as she slithered down into the foot area. Thank God she was a slim child. Now it was Ronnie's job to keep them afloat and faced into the wind.

No paddle to help them, the best Ronnie could do was use the rudder. It helped, but not enough, and the seas were getting rougher. There was no way Seth was going to make shore. Unless he truly was the soulless beast Carol had named him, he'd basically committed suicide.

But he'd seemed confident he could swim the impossible distance to shore, and those men had wanted to kill him...

No. It couldn't be true. Seth might have strange eyes, but the man she knew was far from soulless. She should never have doubted him at Carol's. But having the man you love suddenly described as soulless when you were trapped together and people were out to get you...what was she saying? There was no excuse for what she'd done. And now he was gone, and unless he *really* was soulless, she and Maddy were in this alone and she had to get them out of it.

The night turned black around them and rain started to fall. To the west, three huge cruise ships made a stately procession up the inside passage, their lights like Christmas trees reflected in the rain and on the water. But the camouflaged men had chosen well if they'd intended to abandon them where they wouldn't easily be found. She could imagine the story: Seth's insane girlfriend/employee somehow overpowers and kills her boss and then takes her daughter with her when she tries to get rid of the body. They go too far out on the water without wearing PFDs and an accident happens and they lose their paddles. The rest is tragic history.

She almost wished she was back with Jared. At least Maddy would have a chance, then. She might be damaged, but she'd be alive.

She shook herself from where she'd slumped. Holy heck, thoughts like that were sure signs that she'd almost lost her coherence—a sign that hypothermia was setting in. No way in heck would Jared be better for Maddy. Her daughter deserved the freedom to be what she wanted to be, to grow into an independent woman.

But the kayak prow kept falling away before the wind, and the rudder was a hopeless instrument. She tried paddling with her hands, but succeeded only in freezing her fingers. There was only one thing she could think of to hold the kayak in position and that was to have something like a sea anchor that would hold the rear of the kayak back and thus stop it from turning into the wind. There was only one way she could think of to provide that stability.

She leaned forward and twisted her hands through the cords that laced the central cargo hold, then pulled her legs out of the cockpit.

Seth would likely say she was a fool, but the wind was increasing and the waves were growing in size.

She straddled the hull behind the cockpit and nearly slipped overboard when the wind caught her full force. When she grabbed hold of the cockpit, the wind's drag on the kayak almost took the whole thing over with her. She threw herself on her belly, then worked her body back along the stern of the kayak, wrapped her hands in the bungee cords on the stern cargo hold. She let her body slip back until her legs dragged in the water. This had better work because there was no going back. She didn't have the strength to haul herself back in.

The cords tightened around her wrists, but with her legs dragging in the water, her chilled flesh barely felt the pain.

Chapter 13

Black water sleeked over Seth as he headed toward the place in the ocean that his Selkie brain told him were Ronnie's coordinates. He knew where he'd left her. He knew the currents—far better than even the Coast Guard, who would right now be deploying their Marine Search and Rescue team from Gibsons Harbor. That meant Ronnie had a chance. Even if his weary body didn't get there first.

He popped his head up and read the stars. As they should be, but whitecaps smashed their heads against him. The kayak had to be just there—southwest. He was sure of it from his revised sense of magnetic north. He snuffled the air and sure enough, his sensitive nose caught her scent amid the brine-swirled air. The rain sleeted sideways so there was no protection at all in a kayak's open cockpit. He just had to pray that he got there in time. Maddy was a particular worry, she was so small.

He dove again, sleeking through the water just under the churning waves.

Just live, Ronnie, just live, became a litany. His blood carried the prayer pulsing through his flippers and tail. It sang through his veins and filled him with power. The selkie magic healed his wound and he was whole and more powerful than either seal or man.

There—there ahead, a flash of something lighter in the darkness of sea. He surfaced. The silhouette of a light colored kayak rode the waves ahead of the wind. Somehow, miraculously, Ronnie had kept the craft from capsizing. Then he saw the body.

Draped across the kayak stern hung a slim body. Outstretched arms clung limply to the boat, while the legs and lower body trailed in the waves. He surged to the boat and her comatose form. Butted her with his muzzle. She groaned and turned her head toward him.

Alive! She was alive!

And where was Maddy? By all appearances, the front cockpit was empty.

Bones cracked and reformed. Ears grew from the sides of his head. Flippers elongated and tail split apart until he hung naked in the water, draped in a skin of fur.

He grabbed the side of the kayak and hauled himself up. Praise the gods, the cockpit wasn't empty. Maddy curled in on herself in six inches of water. He hauled himself up so he straddled the recalcitrant whale of a kayak.

"Maddy?" He gently touched her shoulder.

She moaned and pulled herself deeper into the cockpit like a human snail. The water in the cockpit couldn't be helped and it was going to get worse with the rain pouring down, but he cracked open the dry bag and pulled out a foil blanket. He wrapped it around Maddy as best he could and prayed her own body heat could save her. It was going to be a close thing. Then he turned himself around, trying not to capsize the kayak that Ronnie had sacrificed herself to keep upright.

The rain slammed into his face in stinging pellets as he slid to the rear cockpit and reached for Ronnie. He caught her wrists and hauled, but her hands were tangled in the bungee lines. Finally, he pulled a knife out of the bag and slashed the cords away from her poor blued flesh.

"By all the gods, Ronnie, what have you done?"

He hauled her up to him and into his arms, her head slumping to his shoulder.

"Live, damn you. Live. I've cost you and Maddy too much already." He wrapped her in another foil blanket and held her to share warmth, but the wind caught the kayak, and without her trailing legs, it kept turning broadside into the wind. Finally, he slipped her into the cockpit where she slumped and then kissed her one last time before he slid into the water. There he pulled a strobe light from the bag and attached it to the center cargo hold where it might be seen. Then he pulled the last item from the bag: a flare.

It lit the sky red when he sent it into the night, praying that the search and rescue spotters he'd called would see its telltale to set their course. The water was frigid. Even he wouldn't last long in human form—not after the labors he'd been through this night. He pulled his sleek fur around him and began his change back into himself. When he'd finished, he looked one last time at Ronnie.

And found her looking back at him.

§

"Seth?" Her voice was lost in the howl of the wind and the roar of the waves. Or maybe it was just that she'd said nothing at all, only thought she had. Because what she'd seen couldn't be true. The man she loved who'd been lost at sea, suddenly transformed into—a seal?

She shook her head and tried to see, but there was nothing there, only angry ocean and wind and clouds thick as soup overhead and glowering down. She shifted and something crackled around her.

Foil blanket? Where did that come from? And hadn't she been half in the water—a sea anchor. That's what she'd been doing. She tried to shove her way out of the blanket, but her hands were useless, painful flippers as if circulation was just returning. And with the foil blanket, she was pretty sure that she was warming up.

But she'd been keeping the kayak straight because the wind kept wanting to blow it sideways. Why wasn't it doing so now even though her upper body made a perfect sail?

She craned around but saw nothing other than lights on the horizon. They jerked across the water. Not horizon. A boat! A searchlight cut the night and stabbed into her eyes. It panned away, and then was back again. Held.

They were found. The nightmare was over!

And Seth?

She had to be mistaken. A seal and a man were not one and the same.

Soon a red zodiac came along side and two orange-clad figures caught hold of the kayak.

"Are you all right?" a voice called from beneath a visored helmet.

"I—I think so. My daughter's in the front cockpit. Is she all right?"

Strong arms fished in the cockpit and came up with a foil-wrapped, blonde-haired prawn.

"Alive and kicking," said a male voice.

Then more strong arms clasped her and hauled her up and over into the zodiac bottom and laid her down with blankets and the foil wrapped around her beside Maddy. They wrapped a tarp over the two of them like a human taco.

Then the big engines roared to life and the zodiac turned toward shore.

And Seth? Seth was lost to the ocean.

In her tarp-wrapped world, she loosed herself to cling to her daughter.

CHAPTER 14

The battering waves rolled over Seth's head as he hung in the water just off shore. He didn't know the place's name, but the small Vancouver Island fishing village sat nestled at the base of the blue folds of mountains on the Pacific side of Vancouver Island—the opposite side of the island and a very long way from the Sunshine Coast. Far enough away it would take a fast-moving fishing boat three days to get here. As a seal, it had taken him almost two weeks with little rest and no sleep, following the ever fainter taint of diesel and the taste of *that* boat in the waves.

It had been so faint over the past twenty-four hours that he could barely believe he'd found his enemy, but the bloom of the incense scent in the water as he'd passed the last rocky headland had confirmed it.

In seal form, he ducked under the heavy swells and made his way toward the breakwater, the dark blue water refreshingly clean after threading through the archipelago of small islands north of here. The water ruffled like fingers through his thick pelt of fur. The currents smelled of deep ocean, forever wild and untamed. An echo of that untamed nature ached in him. Once he'd sought to lose himself in those thunderous deeps. Forget the human side of his life. But not now. Not now when Ronnie had to be avenged.

He had to pray that she and Maddy had been rescued in time. To think of them dying because of him...

He fought back the overwhelming slick of self-loathing and rage that were the precursor to madness. The same madness that had almost killed him at the loss of Gwyneth and Caleb. If Ronnie or Maddy were gone, he truly would lose himself—commit himself to the wild beast instead of the man. Swim away and die that way.

But not now. Now there came retribution.

The water's surge carried him around the man-made breakwater and into the polluted harbor so that he lurked in the shadows of the stone. Far out across the water, the sun laid blood red strands across the sky. It reflected in the water all around him so that the troller he sought and the fleet of other vessels appeared to float in a harbor of blood. Fitting, given who his prey were and what they and their ancestors had done.

Abandoning a woman and a child to drown, when their only crime was to befriend his kind.

There were too many people around the harbor to act now; some worked on boat engines. Some dealt with nets and fishing lines. A few gathered to enjoy a beer beside seven small runabouts hauled up on the shore and a bright blue double kayak. His gaze caught there and he smiled a seal smile as he bided his time. Canines bared as he swam deep and caught fish, rending the sweet-salty flesh to refuel his depleted strength. He rested beneath the waves, resurfacing briefly again and again to catch his breath and spy on the village.

Smoke rose from chimneys of the drab-colored houses huddled by the water or set back in the trees. On a rocky promontory at one end of the village was a large, log home with large windows that caught and held the bloody light until it faded. The place's opulence didn't fit with the village. He ducked back beneath the waves and slid through the harbor. Inside the breakwater, the water was dark and thick with the sludgy murk of boat sewer and spilled diesel, both foul against his sensitive eyes and muzzle and the too-recent scar on his side.

He came up near the house and inhaled. Even inside the harbor the waves were increasing as the light fell and salt spray filled his face. The swirling wind brought the too-sweet scent of church incense. The descendant of Jacob Ryan was here.

How many years had this man pursued him, had the church pursued him? It was over fifty years since Gwyneth and Caleb had died and he had lost himself, most of that time lost as seal deep in the ocean. How they had tracked him was a wonder, but then fate was a strange thing, and fate had brought him and this man together just as it had brought him and Ronnie together. It was a chance to put things to right. A second chance for the world to find balance and for him to find peace—even if he and Ronnie could never be together.

The sun fell beyond the edge of the world and darkness flooded from beneath the tall cedars. The glowing lights of the houses spilled out their windows and pooled around the village, providing succor in a cold dark world. But light hadn't saved his family. It hadn't saved his kind.

He waited just off the promontory for the night to deepen. Gradually, the lights of the village vanished and the darkness of the beginning of the world slipped in amongst the houses. Overhead a thick layer of cloud had caught against the tops of the mountains and rain started to fall in thick, fat drops that picked up speed. The rain had increased to a wind-driven deluge when he finally stripped off his seal skin and stepped from the water. Rain sluiced the salt away as he tied his skin around his hips. His human skin tingled, the wind almost painful. The rush of air carried the scent of cedar and salt brine but could not mask the stink of incense.

Lightly, he climbed the granite promontory. The last light had gone out in the log house as he slunk to its front porch with its deep wicker chairs intended for loungers enjoying the view. He sniffed the cushions and knew Jacob Ryan's descendant had sat here, enjoying his world and contemplating having dealt with his enemy.

Seth growled and crossed to the door. He tried the lock and the door swung open—such was trust in this village. He had once had such a home himself. The wind caught the door and he leapt to catch it before it slammed against the interior wall. A well of darkness waited beyond.

And the scent of church incense almost caustic in his lungs.

He stepped across the threshold into a two-story foyer and pulled the door shut behind him. The rain pounded the roof and splattered the windows. The sound of the waves was a dull roar from outside. Nothing moved in the house, but two hearts beat from rooms upstairs.

Cold tiles lay underfoot. Dead logs made up the walls. He swallowed at the sudden sense of claustrophobia the place evoked even with its high ceilings. A tangle of Wellington boots and sneakers lay beside the door and an antique coat rack held Gore-Tex jackets and slickers. Fishermen's wear.

Silently he checked the rooms to either side of the foyer. A living room on one side, an office on the other. He scanned the maps and photos framed on the office walls. One held stick pins in it and he crossed to it. Red and black pins spread along the world's shorelines. He stopped. A black pin had been pressed into the small indentation that was the Sunshine Coast. Another sat along the north Irish coast where once he'd loved a woman named Gwyneth. There had been a town there once. Now, he knew, there were only ruins.

Did the black pins indicate places where the Ryans had destroyed his people? Did that mean the red pins were places where his people might still exist? A small seed of hope sprouted in his chest. Perhaps he wasn't alone, the last of his kind. He scanned the map again, committing it to memory, and then left the room.

But he would eventually be the last if this man was allowed to continue his crusade against the Selkie.

He crossed to the kitchen and pulled a knife from a block, then climbed the stairs to the second floor. Wind smeared the rain against the broad front windows. The roof shuddered and groaned. Swiftly he went down the hallway to the first closed door. A single heartbeat beyond.

He slid the door open and peered in on a child's bedroom full of spaceship models and computer games. A boy of perhaps seven years slept, his arms wide in abandon. The structure of his face said whose child he was.

Seth grimly stepped back into the hall and closed the door behind him. He would not emulate the inhuman beast that Ryan's descendant was.

Knife at his side, he continued down the hall toward a set of double doors at the end. Five steps before he reached them, one door swung open and a male figure clad in pajamas and a robe stepped out.

The air flared with incense as their gazes met. Seth and the man froze.

"You," Jacob Ryan's descendant said. Then his gaze found the butcher knife in Seth's hand and his eyes widened. "You're supposed to be dead."

Seth shrugged. "You got me in the side, Ryan—it is Ryan, isn't it? I made it to my skin."

Ryan snarled. "And now what? You've come for revenge?"

Seth shook his head. "To end it. Between you and me, at least." He lifted his chin at the door. "Where's your wife?"

"No wife. The bitch left me, so I took the boy." The man's eyes gained an ugly flare as if anything female was loathed.

"Just like Jacob Ryan. It must run in the family."

Ryan lunged for Seth and grabbed for the knife, but Seth leapt aside and drove the hilt of the blade into the side of the man's skull. He staggered and fell against the wall. Seth caught Ryan's right arm and twisted it behind him, then shoved him back into his bedroom. Large. Sprawling. A king-sized bed, covers tangled and the reek of unwashed clothing.

Seth shoved him to the bed and tossed a fallen pair of trousers and a shirt at him. "Get dressed."

"Why should I?"

Seth held up the knife. "Because if you don't, I'll use this—and not just on you."

It was an empty threat, but this man—this creature—didn't know that. And in Seth's long life, he'd learned that people judge the truth of your words by what they would do themselves. Jacob Ryan's descendant had already proved that, for him, the life of innocents meant nothing.

"Leave my boy out of this. He knows nothing of any of it."

Perhaps it was true, but this man had perpetuated the hate of his father and he must have been very young when Seth's family had been killed.

"The men who helped you. Where are they?"

Ryan's descendant shook his head as he pulled his trousers up over his pajamas. "How the hell do I know? The church sent them. Mercenaries, I think. I'm just a tracker." He shoved his arms through his sleeves and shrugged on his shirt. "I don't know what you're planning, but whatever happens to me, they'll know you were behind it. They'll come for you."

"But you said it yourself. I'm already dead." Seth smiled, almost taking too much pleasure in the other man's discomfort. Desperation talked that way. It just didn't work.

Around them the house shuddered in the wind. Seth nodded at the bedroom door. "That way. We're taking a little walk."

He caught the man's arm again and twisted it back until they were forced into lockstep for the trip down the hall, down the stairs, and into the foyer. He released the man again.

"Put on boots and a coat." Best leave the place looking like Ryan planned to go out.

The man obeyed and Seth shoved him out the front door.

Rain and wind slammed into them, though they were still sheltered on the porch. The rain-slicked wood was slippery underfoot as they went down the stairs and then followed a path through salal and juniper around the house to the narrow lane into town. Trees thrashed and groaned in the wind. Branches crashed to the ground and the air was full of needles and reeked of fir and cedar. A river of water flowed down the dirt road and into the main road to the village. Seth shoved Ryan before him, down through the darkened houses. Down toward the harbor.

"If I yell, people will come running. They might not know the monster you are, but they'll still help me," Ryan's descendant said through the rain.

Seth shook his head, his adrenaline pinging in his limbs. With all the days of swimming, he needed this to be over, and soon. Adrenaline would only last so long. "You could, but you won't. This is between you and me—this ending. One or the other of us will die and then it will be over."

They reached the pier, with its cadre of tethered seiners and trollers huddled against the wind and waves. Through the dark came the crash of the rollers against the stone breakwater. Not a good night to be out at all. Seth shoved him down the pier to the boat that had almost carried Ronnie and Maddy to their deaths. He quickly slipped the lines holding the boat in place and shoved the man onto the deck.

"Start the engines."

The man hesitated, looking out to the sea. "This isn't a good idea."

Seth barely glanced at him; instead he scanned the deck for weapons. The craft was neatly kept, with coiled ropes and stowed nets. Everything in its place, including the storage locker that had held the three of them prisoner.

"It wasn't a good idea for a woman and a child to be out in heavy weather in a kayak either, but they were. With no paddles either. Maybe I can do the same for you."

Ryan lunged and caught Seth in the gut with his shoulder.

Seth's breath oomphed out of him as he was driven into the rail. He felt ribs crack as Ryan grabbed Seth's knife hand and tried to flip him over the rail. Seth held on as Ryan slammed his knife hand against the metal railing. Seth's hand went numb. He took a chance. Released the boat and drove his fist into Ryan's gut, clawed at his face.

Ryan fell back and Seth stumbled upright on the slick deck. He still had the knife, but his arm tingled and felt as useful as a rubber weapon. From somewhere Ryan produced a fish gaff. He swung at Seth's head.

Seth ducked and the weapon followed, slamming on his already compromised arm. His arm went completely numb and the knife clattered to the deck.

Both of them leapt for it.

Seth reached the knife first, but came out on the bottom, Ryan on his back. The gaff came down on his head and slammed his face into the deck. Darkness ate consciousness. It was over. All his struggles. The only good thing that had come from it had been saving Ronnie and Maddy.

But Ryan might go back for them.

He thrashed under Ryan and managed to roll. Slashed, half-blind, with the knife in his numb hand and felt the blade slice through something.

Rain poured into his face, half blinding him as he peered up into Ryan's descendant's face. The man had dropped the gaff and now used both hands to force Seth's knife back toward him. Through the darkness, Seth saw the blade's gleam and the glint in Ryan's gaze.

"Tables are turned now, ya filthy beast," Ryan growled.

Seth fought his other hand free and clawed at Ryan's face. The knife inched closer and he used both hands to keep it from his chest. He had to do something or he was going to end up like the old man—gutted on the sand.

He bucked under Ryan. Bucked again and twisted and threw the weight of his knife arm sideways. Rolled, and suddenly the knife was loose again, skittering across the deck. Ryan was up faster. Seth scrambled up, fumbling for the fish gaff, turning in time to see the man lunge for him with the blade. Seth sidestepped the lunge and kicked at his attacker.

His foot connected with the other man's knee as he drove the gaff across Ryan's shoulders. Seth heard the crack and the scream as the man windmilled his arms and went down, slamming headfirst into the hull rail.

He lay there.

The rain slicked down Seth's naked skin as the feeling in his arm returned. Ryan still hadn't moved. He nudged the man's leg with his foot.

Still nothing.

The knife blade gleamed dully on the deck and Seth tossed it overboard. Holding the gaff as a weapon, he rolled Ryan over. His eyes were wide. His head lolled unnaturally.

Seth checked for a pulse, then sat on his heels and let the reality sink in. It was over, hopefully. Perhaps he and this man's descendants could break out of the anger and fear that had held them prisoner for generations.

He left the dead man on the deck and started the ship's engine, then eased the vessel out of the harbor and into the wind.

It was a rough ride away from the village and rougher still beyond the sheltering islands out into the dark north Pacific Ocean. The waves grew in size the farther he went. Huge rollers hit the hull and rolled over the side, leaving the deck awash in water. The body floated amid the mess of ropes and nets until he was far out and the hump of Vancouver Island was barely visible through the darkness. Then he set the troller's course into the wind, braced open doors and windows, and dragged the body below deck into the engine room before slipping back into the water with the metal gaff in hand.

There, he patiently pried holes in the hull and listened to the burp and gurgle as the water began to fill the engine room.

When he was done, he pulled his skin around him and watched as the troller began to list, then list more steeply until the waves caught it. Waves rolled over the deck and poured below until suddenly the craft upended and the Pacific swallowed it whole.

Seth hung in the waves, feeling the tug as the hungry deeps slurped the fishing boat down. It had felt like this when his first family had died, except he was the thing being drawn into the deep.

Now it was over. At least for this enemy.

He dove under the waves and started southward where he knew the hump of Vancouver Island ended and opened into the more peaceful Georgia Straight where Ronnie and Maddy could now be safe. Soon, when he came up for air , an apricot dawn silhouetted the mountains.

CHAPTER 15

The heat of the late afternoon sun stopped Ronnie one more time as she sluiced water over a kayak at the Coastal Kayak dock. The sun beat down, but it still hadn't managed to warm the chilled part inside of her from that night over a year ago. The blue harbor water glittered and gleamed. The clatter, music, and delicious odors of the town restaurants poured down in a confetti confection of sound and scents. Gulls cried overhead in what might be hunger, but that had become a requiem for a man she'd realized too late that she'd loved. It might have been a fledgling love, but it had been love just the same.

And it was lost now.

"Mommy, you're sighing again. Is something the matter?" Maddy asked from the picnic table Ronnie had set up by the storage shed so that Maddy would have someplace to color while Ronnie worked her long hours. It was easy to work long hours when you owned your own business.

Owned. She, Ronnie Baxter, owned a business, all due to Seth's kindness. When she and Maddy had been recovered from the ocean, they'd been rushed to the hospital; and somewhere in the haze of activity and giving a statement to the police, someone had found a packet of papers on a lanyard inside Ronnie's clothing. Those papers had been a will and a deed to the property that Seth had owned, both signed in his strong hand: the cove house and the kayaking business at Gibsons Landing, hers. Sometime during the month or so they'd known each other, Seth Cullen had seen a lawyer and drafted the papers. At first the police had looked at her with suspicion, but when no one had contested the documents and then a man had disappeared on Vancouver Island leaving behind files that suggested he'd been stalking Seth Cullen, then the police had backed off and the courts had said that she and Maddy could live in the home and run the business while the search continued for the missing man. To date, no body had ever been found, and in her heart she believed it never would.

She didn't want to think about him floating facedown in the ocean, but it was the most likely scenario, regardless of her nightly dreams of him. Regardless of the hypothermia-induced memories of him. Strong arms. A warm hand. A soft kiss. A face in the water, transforming.

They told her that she and Maddy had been found wrapped in foil blankets and that a strobe on the kayak and a flare had led the search and rescue team to them. But there'd been no such thing aboard when they'd been dumped into the middle of Georgia Strait.

How it had happened she didn't know, but in her dreams she was certain Seth had saved them.

She opened her eyes to the music of the harbor—boats rumbling away from the docks, the summer people loading their belongings onto the water taxi to Keats Island. She nodded at Maddy. "Sorry. I guess it's the same old thing as always. I was thinking about Seth."

Maddy nodded. "I wish he'd come back. I liked him a lot. And Roscoe misses him, too. Have you noticed? He's not keeping his fur as nice as he always did."

It was an amazingly adult observation, but then her daughter had always been amazing. She'd been just as amazing when she'd told the family court judge that she did not wish to see her father unless Jared came to visit her here in Canada. In the face of a child who, the child psychologists had said, had not been tampered with by Ronnie, wonder of wonders, the courts in BC and Chicago had awarded her sole custody with only supervised access once a year for Jared. The divorce papers had been drawn up and signed and she—she had her life back, or a new life to begin.

All thanks to Seth Cullen and the strength he'd helped her find.

"I don't think Seth's ever coming back, sweetie. I think we lost him for good that night as sea."

Maddy raised an eyebrow and shook her head. "Well, Roscoe doesn't think so. That's why he spends his afternoons watching the ocean. Sometimes I watch with him, but all I've seen are a couple of killer whales and a seal." She focused on her coloring.

Ronnie shook her head. To live in the magical world of childhood again. What a wonder that would be, to have the people she loved come back from the dead. To have dragons slain and foes vanquished.

But hey, her life had turned out pretty good. Jared slapped down and Carol Dermott mysteriously leaving town had all helped ease Ronnie's settling into Gibsons. She turned off the water and coiled the hose, then eased her back against the strain of work.

"So I think we're done for the day and it's time to head home to Roscoe and Prince Benito." The latter being Maddy's half-grown Maine coon cat, who was quickly getting to a size where Roscoe might have met his match—if the two hadn't become best friends from the time the tiny kitten joined their home. His adoption had been an attempt to fill the void left in the house.

Maddy packed up her crayons and coloring book while Ronnie grabbed her purse and the bag of fresh crab she'd bought at the pier. Maddy raced her up the dock to the shop, and Ronnie would have won, but she had to lock the dock gate. At the shop Ronnie checked the voicemail for any kayak reservations and then they piled into her Civic and headed home. It would be a light meal of salad and crab and an early night because they had a kayaking group going out first thing tomorrow. Maddy would spend the morning at a local daycamp because she'd become friends with other kids her age.

After dinner and a bedtime story with Maddy, Ronnie took a long bath and then sank into the bed that Seth had provided her a lifetime ago. She still had not had the nerve to do more than venture to his end of the house. When she had, she'd had to stop when her knees went weak at his lingering scent of brine and cedar. She'd closed the door to his room behind her, but still found reasons to visit from time to time and breathe in that vestige of him.

The soft bed enveloped her and she curled onto her side. Sleep took her quickly into a sea of dreams.

Black water and tall cliffs. A stone village by the sea. A people there, working, smiling, happy. In the harbor floated fishing boats, but their engines were rarely used. Instead, nets were pulled through the water by strong, sleek beasts with silver-black skins. When they came to the shore, they were transformed to handsome men who hauled in their catch and took fish home to the families who waited. Then came the fear, and the village burned.

Ronnie groaned in her sleep and the image faded. Rolled over and there were waves again, sliding away from her in all directions, and she was frozen and lost and giving up hope. Then Seth was beside her, his strong gentle hands freeing hers, his arms surrounding her with his warm living scent of brine and cedar.

How had he come to be there?

She'd seen, hadn't she? Seth in the water and then his ears had sunk back and become part of his skull. His black hair had shortened and become silver-gray and it was no longer Seth beside her. Instead a great bull seal had hung on the waves beside her. Before it dove it had looked at her with Seth's amber-dark eyes.

Eyes are the window to the soul.

Soulless beast.

No. No, dammit, if there was anyone she knew who had a soul, it was Seth.

She bolted upright, her heart hammering in her chest. Something was happening. Something—was…

She threw back the covers and went to the window. Silver moonlight lit the forest, but like a shadow, something sleeked across the patio, the moonlight catching on moon-silvered fur.

Roscoe, gone to moonlight and shadow in the night.

Something had his attention and he was headed for the water. Men come again to finish her and Maddy?

Pulling on sneakers and a sweater over her shorty pajamas, she headed for the patio door and stepped out into the cool wind off the water. The hushed sound of waves came from the cove, but nothing more; and there was no sign of Roscoe, but something felt— wrong. Her heart hammered in her chest so hard there was no denying that something wasn't right. The night had gone still and watchful, all but the ocean because the water never slept. A huckleberry bush trembled at the edge of the woods.

"Roscoe? Come here, now buddy." Of course the big cat didn't oblige. Instead Prince Benito wrapped his fur around her bare legs and she nearly fainted in surprise. She leaned down to pat him. "What's going on, Benny? Huh?"

Her voice sounded overloud. The moon threw shifting shadows under the trees and all the little hairs on her body prickled in warning.

The crunch of gravel turned her around as two figures came around the end of the house. A sound behind her and another man blocked that direction.

"Hello, Ronnie." It was Jared's voice. "I've come to take back what belongs to me."

Prince Benito growled low down in his throat. Ronnie leapt for the door and slammed it closed, then ran for the phone. Picked it up and stabbed 9-1-1, but nothing happened. The line was dead. Her purse. Her cell. Where were they? Maddy had taken to playing games on the phone. She ran for the bedrooms just as something smashed the sliding glass door open. Glass crashed to the floor.

Maddy woke up screaming.

Ronnie ran into Maddy's room and slammed and locked the door behind her, grabbed Maddy, and there was her cell on the bedside table. She grabbed it, too, and headed for the window. Just get out into the woods and Jared wouldn't find them. She slid the window up as someone threw themselves against the door. Maddy screamed again.

"Maddy, it's me. It's Daddy!" came from beyond the door.

"Daddy?" Maddy squirmed in Ronnie's arms.

"Hush, baby. We need to get away. Your daddy wants to take you away. If he does, we'll never see each other again. Do you understand?"

Maddy looked up at her with owl-shaped eyes as Ronnie helped her out the window.

The pounding on the door continued. Ronnie leapt down and dragged Maddy across to the woods.

"But it's Daddy, Mommy."

"I know, honey. Come on."

A crash sounded from the house as the door obviously broke. Jared's voice rose in a howl from the room when he discovered they were gone.

"I'll kill you, you bitch! You can't have my daughter!"

Ronnie carried Maddy into the forest, the trees sighing and tall around her. The wind shifting the leaves to hide her path. She hoped.

She fumbled the phone up and hit 9-1-1. The call tone drilled into her ear.

"9-1-1. What is your emergency?" the operator said.

"My ex-husband is here. He's threatening to kill me and take my daughter," she whispered.

"What's your address, please?"

Her address. Her mind drew a blank. She looked to the trees and back toward the house. Jared was standing in the bushes looking right at her.

"No!" She turned and ran, Maddy in her arms.

In three strides, Jared had her by the shoulder and spun her around. His backhand took her in the face and she staggered back and fell. Her phone skittered away and she lay shocked and stunned. Then the pain made her head swim and he snatched Maddy from her as his men came up to join him.

Fighting the pain, she scrambled to her knees. No way was he taking her baby from her, but she couldn't seem to stand.

"Take her. I've got some teaching to do to this one." He handed a shrieking, fighting Maddy to one of his men and buried a booted foot in Ronnie's side.

All her air oofed out of her. She collapsed on her shoulder and the night went black. It was happening again and it could not be happening. It could not!

"You do not." Another boot. "Mess with me."

Another boot. "You do not." Another boot. "Steal my daughter from me."

Ronnie curled into herself against the pain, trying to protect her stomach, her face. Jared wasn't having that. He grabbed her hair and hauled her up.

"Are you listening?" His fist came back. Here were the blows she remembered. Here were the blows she couldn't protect herself from. There was nothing she could do.

Except there was. This was Maddy they were talking about. Everything depended on what she did. She reached up and clawed his face.

When he bellowed, she yanked away and staggered back, glaring.

"I'm listening, you sick little man. If you're going to kill me anyway, I might as well say what I've always been thinking. You're a sad, sick joke of a man if you think beating on a woman gives you power. You might be able to kill me, but you can't scare me anymore."

His fist plowed into her face and sent her head rocking back. Her legs gave, and from somewhere there was Maddy, screaming, and a yowl. Something dark and silver hurtled through the forest. Something snarled and leapt at Jared's men.

One man went down, clutching at his throat and gasping for breath. The other held Maddy to him like a shield and backed toward the house.

Jared yelled and suddenly he no longer towered over her. She scrambled up as stars blazed in her eyes and blood roared in her ears.

Maddy. Where was Maddy? She stumbled up.

"What the hell! Fucking animals!" a man yelled and Maddy screamed again.

Ronnie stumbled through the woods seeking her baby. And there she was, against the house while Prince Benito was wrapped around the man's head and Roscoe darted in to tear at his legs.

She scooped Maddy up and ran for her car, just as sirens blared and turned down her driveway. Red and blue strobes lit the sides of the trees. The cars stopped and four police officers greeted her.

"He's—he's back there. Roscoe and Benito stopped his men. Something kn-kn-knocked Jared aside and I got free."

An officer guided her to the rear of the car and wrapped her and Maddy in a blanket. An ambulance came and tended to her face and head. She hadn't even realized she was bleeding from her nose, a cut lip, and a large piece of missing scalp.

A few minutes later the police came back, each guiding a man. One had scratch marks around his face. Another held his shirt to his neck, and a third stumbled after them, his face a mass of welts and bruises.

"I found this one already trussed in the bushes. You know anything about that?" asked the officer, indicating Jared.

Ronnie shook her head.

The ambulance took Ronnie and Maddy to the hospital where they were once more checked over and the officers questioned them. When they were released, it was daylight and there was no way in the world Ronnie could lead a tour this morning. Aside from weariness and sore stitches, her body was seizing up from cracked ribs and all the bruising.

She called one of her tour leaders and made arrangements, then she and Maddy went home to check on Roscoe and Prince Benito.

The found both cats sunning themselves on the patio beyond the pool of shattered patio door glass. Maddy she put to bed for a nap and then she busied herself sweeping up the glass.

Something did not compute and she needed to think about that. Someone had trussed up Jared and someone or something had come to her rescue last night, along with Prince Benito and Roscoe. Roscoe, who'd been headed for the cove when she'd seen him through her window.

There had been something silver and black who had come for her, while Roscoe and Benito helped Maddy.

She finished sweeping the glass into the dustbin and stood, easing her back as she stared through the trees at the water.

The sweet cedar- and pine-scented air swept around her on a small breeze. The waves made a gentle murmur from down on the cove. Roscoe looked up at her with sleepy eyes, licked a paw, and then settled for more dozing as if he'd earned it. Prince Benito looked up and gave a hopeful chirrup as if hoping for his breakfast.

She reached down to pat him. "In a few minutes, my big, brave Benny."

She set off down the path to the water and came around a stand of huckleberry and looked out at the cove, still hugging herself against the morning's marine chill.

Gentle waves lapped the shore as Ronnie looked over the water. There was something there. Something large and dark sleeked under the surface, but the angled sunlight caught on silver.

All the little hairs rose on Ronnie's neck and she was tempted to take refuge in the house, but she had to know. She had to see for herself what she'd only fully seen in her dreams so far. She had to understand what held her here in Gibsons, because it was more than simply a house and business. There was something deep inside her hoping, yearning.

A dark, blunt-muzzled head broke the surface and peered shoreward with dark eyes, just as hundreds of seals did along the coast every day.

She stepped down to the water as the creature cruised closer.

"Seth? I know it's you. Please show yourself." Her whisper sounded overloud in the stillness.

The creature—surely only a seal—snuffed at the water and dove under the surface.

What the heck was she doing? Seth was gone, drowned, and all her hopes were based on half-delirious dreams of a beaten woman and a woman who had been too far gone with hypothermia to be coherent. Just go back to the house and call a glazier and a carpenter and then go to bed.

Instead she stepped into the water so it soaked into her shoes.

"Seth? Thank you for saving us last night. And a year ago. Thank you for the house and the business, but what I really want is you. Have you come back to me?"

The creature's head reappeared closer. Then the creature's blunt muzzle sank back and became a nose, fur faded away and became a man's face, wet, dark hair falling over the forehead. Then he stood up in the water and threw back the silver-gray seal skin. Seth in all his splendor, naked muscles rippling in the golden rays of early morning sunlight, the water gleaming on his abs and broad shoulders.

"Seth." She waded deeper toward him.

"I had to see you—at least one more time. I had to know you were okay. Thank God I came to check on you last night," he said. Then he stopped and almost shyly held her green scarf out to her.

And she knew better. "You've been here all along, haven't you? You've been watching out for us."

He wouldn't meet her gaze. "I kept your scarf safe. How's Maddy?"

"Asleep. She's well—sleeping off last night, thanks to you. She—she's been waiting for you to return."

He smiled that most wonderful, even smile and looked down at her.

"And you?" He stroked her cheek. "Did you know your pajama bottoms are getting wet?"

She looked down. She was almost hip deep in water. "I don't care. You're here or this is the most vivid dream I've ever had, and I've dreamed of you a lot this past year. Thank you for everything you've given us, but as I said, what I want is *you*."

Finding bravery she didn't know she had, she reached out and placed a palm on his solid chest. Real. She looked up and met his strange, dark gaze. "I've missed you so much."

He sighed as he nodded. "I want to stay, but the curse of the selkie makes it impossible."

Selkie. Years before on the east coast, she'd heard tales of the mythical seal-men. "What curse?"

"If I love you, I can only stay with you a year and a day. After that the sea will call me back."

Ronnie shook her head. "But surely you can come back again."

He shook his head sadly. "A year and a day. That's all we're allowed. Then the sea will have us."

"But we've already lost a year together." She stepped up to him, swooped the scarf around his neck, and hauled herself into his chest. He was sleek and hard-muscled against her. "I can't lose you again, Seth."

His strong arms came around her and he kissed her hair, her brow, her eyelids. Then his warm mouth trailed down her face and their mouths met. Salt and the sweet yearning a year brought. She pressed herself around him and stretched her arms around his neck, intent on never letting go.

When Seth pulled back with a groan, she was breathless and too aware of the naked man before her and of the dampness of her thin pajamas. Virtually nothing between them and she wanted skin on skin. His dark gaze had gone smoldering with a matching desire.

"Did I tell you that a lot has happened in a year? Carol Dermott is gone. They went to arrest her, but she'd disappeared. And my divorce came through. I'm a free woman—and alive to enjoy it, thanks to you. The police are charging Jared with spousal assault and attempted abduction. They think he'll go away for a long time."

He pulled her into him again. "I don't care about Jared. I care about you and Maddy. You realize that if we do this, we're doomed a year from now."

A year. A precious year. "It's not enough time. I think—I think I could love you for all time, Seth Cullen. Until the seas are gone and the mountains fall down."

He stopped and held her from him studying her eyes. Then he reached behind him for the silver-black skin that floated on the water around him. Swiftly he folded it and held its softness between them.

"There is way..." Tentatively he held the bundled skin out to her. "Take it. If a human hides a selkie skin, the selkie is trapped ashore, the human's prisoner until the selkie finds his skin. Take this and hide it. Hide it well and we can be together."

Horrified, Ronnie fell back a pace. She shoved the skin back at him. "You'd give up the sea for me? How can you say that? I don't want you as my prisoner. You'd always resent me. And what if something happened to me? What then? You'd never get back your skin!"

"I won't resent you. I trust you and I love you. I love you more than the sea itself. Please, Ronnie, help me stay with you. And if you're so worried, leave word with a lawyer about where the skin can be found. It's the only way."

Hesitantly she accepted the skin. Soft. Softer than Roscoe's or Benito's fluffy pelts. Like touching a silken dream—the magical dream that was her life. She shivered and swallowed. "That's why the church wanted to kill your people. You're magical beings—not something their beliefs can allow."

He nodded and she looked down at the skin she held. "All right. On one condition. If you ever feel that things aren't working, you're to tell me and I'll return the skin."

Seth just looked at her. "And you promise me that if things aren't working, you'll return the skin and send me packing."

"Won't those men come looking for you again? Won't you be helpless without your skin?"

He pulled her into his arms again, the softness of his skin between them. "I took care of them. After what they did to you and Maddy, they won't be coming back. And I'll never be helpless as long as you're at my side."

And then he kissed her once more, passionately, deeply, as his hands found the elastic top of her pajama bottoms and slid inside to cup her bottom.

Ronnie pressed into him, wanting him now, but then she pulled away from him, leaving her scarf trailing from his neck.

"Hold that thought, but I've got a skin to hide. Don't go anywhere. I've always had fantasies of making love in water."

Then she was dashing up the shore for the trees, wracking her brain for a hiding place that would keep Seth Cullen with her for a very long time.

Join K.L. Abrahamson's Romance Readers

If you'd like to read more of Karen L. Abrahamson's paranormal romance and romantic suspense, join other romance readers and receive two free romance novels.

To get your free books, go to www.karenlabrahamson.com and join Karen's romance readers email list.

Don't go yet. Please leave a review!

If you enjoyed this book (and even if you didn't), it would be immensely helpful if you would leave a review at your favorite on-line retailer or on Goodreads. Reviews help gain me visibility and they can bring my books to the attention of other readers who may enjoy them.

Thank you!

About the Author

Karen L. Abrahamson is a well-traveled writer who has explored cultures and countries around the world but British Columbia, Canada is her favorite place to come back to. She is the author of literary, mystery, romantic and fantasy fiction including the *Unlocking (Peachland) Series* involving six women, a mysteriously powerful bracelet, danger and romance. She lives on the west coast of Canada with eagles, bears and killer whales for neighbors.

When she isn't writing she can be found with a camera and backpack in fabulous locations around the world.

To find out more about her and her writing, visit

www.karenlabrahamson.com

Fantasy and Romance by

Karen L. Abrahamson

Romance

Second Spring
Judas Kiss
Coming Down Christmas
Shades of Moonlight
Shadow Play
Ashes and Light

Unlocking Her Heart
Unlocking Her History
Unlocking Her Grace
Unlocking Her Dreams
Unlocking Her Chances
Unlocking Her Doubts

Surviving Safe Harbor

Fantasy

The Warden of Power
Impossible
The Cartographer's Daughter
The American Geological Survey Series:
Afterburn
Aftershock
Aftermath
Afterimage

Terra Incognita
Terra Infirma
Terra Nueva

Other Fantasy Novels

Ice Dragon
Emberstone
Mutable Things
The Crystal Courtesan

A Special Sneak Peak

of

Unlocking Her Heart

Chapter 1

Kylee Jensen drove her car toward the edge of a cliff.

At least that was what it felt like. The descent went on forever, so steep that even though she took her foot off the gas, the old silver Honda Civic continued to pick up speed until she was practically standing on the brake *all the time* even though she knew the car's brakes probably couldn't take it. They'd been squealing even before she left Vancouver for the Okanagan via the Coquihalla Highway but now it was like the brake pads didn't want to be in a relationship at all, and she was terrifyingly free-wheeling it.

The steep hill had stripped her from the top of Pennask Summit, down from the treed tops of the mountains through noon-day sunshine, following the side of a long valley that led to some place invisible below and eastward. The valley's steep sides were green with pine, here and there stained lighter with what must be poplar or aspen, still carrying their spring shade this early in June. Scars cut into the treescape marked logging roads that ran even more steeply down the mountainsides. That was it. She was flipping driving herself off the side of a *mountain* and whose silly idea was it coming here anyway?

She tromped the brakes again and a horrible squeal filled the cab of the car. Figured. She was going to go careening over the side of the road, and the burned-out brakes and the stink of metal on metal would be a fitting metaphor for the way her whole darn life had gone full-on out of control. Actually, the whole darn mad slide was a symbol of her life—chasing after something she could never quite catch up to, until she was running wild toward disaster after disaster.

Yup. That was Kylee Jensen, all right. Relationship Typhoid Mary.

The road curved around a bend and sunlight through the trees banded the four lanes of pavement. A black shape burst up in front of her car and she had a momentary image of wings and huge black beak and eyes.

What the heck? She jerked the car sideways and slammed on the brakes again. The shriek shrilled through the car and she careened to a stop at the side of the highway and sat there shaking in sudden silence. Her chest tightened and she wanted to cry.

Darn it, she was better than this. Bigger than this. It was a crow. A single crow. Sure, it was the biggest darned crow she'd ever seen, but it was only a bird and this was just a road that cars and even logging trucks drove down every single day. It was *her* that was out of control. The trucks and cars had been passing her for the last five miles of the trip, so obviously she wasn't going to drive off the cliff, if she kept her head about her and babied her car. She had to baby the car. It was the last thing larger than a suitcase that she owned in the world. Heck, she could end up living in the darn thing if things didn't work out in Peachland.

So enough sitting here feeling sorry for herself. She dropped the car into gear and pulled out onto the road again. It really had been the *biggest* darn crow she'd ever seen.

Was it a bad omen of what awaited ahead?

It was a bird. Think of it as a phoenix symbolizing her finding a new life out of the ashes of what had come before. She snorted. Grasping at straws much?

The road curved again and ahead the steep-sided valley she'd been following opened up to reveal a distant dry mountainside. At least that looked familiar, like the hills on the far side of Okanagan Lake.

As if on cue, the road curved again and flattened out, and then the car climbed up to a long flat stretch that revealed the massive lake—almost 84 miles long she'd once been told— stretched north to south below her. Its blue water was the same shade as the sky, its waves glitter-topped with sunlight. Beautiful and cool and welcoming compared with the heat through her windshield. Just down one more hill and she'd be there.

To the right of the highway, the land dropped down to small pastures, orchards and vineyards. This was the heart of British Columbia's wine and orchard country, though the old family orchards were too quickly being turned into vineyards or housing developments. She took the sharp turnoff for Peachland and joined the highway that ducked down steep treed bluffs toward the water. In places the trees were replaced by a stunning growth in building. Broad swathes of houses filled the hillside. Other areas where orchards had been, now held fancy houses between the highway and the water. Not what she'd expected.

Peachland, just by its name was supposed to be a sleepy little village that curved in a long string of cottages and houses along the waterside of a large bay. It was supposed to be surrounded by rolling orchards full of huge ripening peaches. Why else would it have that name? But this—this was like it was a suburb or something and if she wanted a suburb she could have stayed in Vancouver. Or Seattle. She had her green card. Maybe she should just turn the old Civic around and head back home. Or where home once had been, once upon a time when Kevin was in her life. Get real, Kylee. That was just the most recent place you lived. None of them have ever truly been home.

Her throat tightened as she fought off the tears. Her fists clenched on the steering wheel. A small shopping center with a grocery store, gas station, liquor store and library sprang up on her right and a stoplight interrupted the highway traffic.

Okay, maybe this wasn't the big city, because where in the big city world did you ever see highway traffic stopped by a stoplight. Nope, that was definitely small town. She clicked on her turn signal and glanced down at the open address book on the seat next to her.

Fifteen-twenty Beach Avenue. It evoked images of sand and blue water and friends on beach towels. It evoked memories of her friend Lila so long ago when they'd been kids in high school and had taken a trip up here to visit Lila's grandparents. They'd been fifteen then and she was thirty now. Thirty going on a hundred and forty and her life felt like it was over. Again.

She turned left onto Beach Avenue and found herself on the lakeshore: a narrow strip of public beach, shady weeping willows, picnic tables and park benches separating her from the water. Here and there people had towels spread across the pea-gravel beach and were sunning themselves just like she remembered. She smiled and the tension from the drive evaporated just like the heat haze over the water.

She pulled a u-turn and parked the car in a shady spot across from the beach and climbed out. Peachland was no longer quite so small, but it was still strung along the lakefront. She'd been driving for three and a half hours and really could use the chance to stretch her legs. Besides, it would give her a chance to 'sess out the town and decide just how crazy she was to come here. Lila could have sold her grandparent's house and moved on. They hadn't been in touch in a long time except for a few postcards Kylee had sent from overseas. But no. Lila loved the old house by the lake. She was loyal.

The wind off the lake ruffled her pixy-cut short blonde hair and played at the hem of her floral travel dress. It was one of the few things she had left that didn't look totally worn and drab from travel. She'd bought it on the spur of the moment with the foolish belief that Kevin and she might get married somewhere on their trip. After all, they'd been engaged two years before they left on the trip of a lifetime. She'd thought that this time things really were right.

Well, that was *another* lifetime. Certainly not this one. She spun on her ballet-flat heel and started walking, her trusty daypack over her shoulder. The breeze wafted scents of suntan lotion and barbecue picnics. Out on the lake, a powerboat hauled two laughing kids on an inner tube and closer to shore two kayakers glided like ghosts over the water. Voices called to each other, laughed. An elderly couple smiled and said hello as they passed her, walking hand in hand along the promenade. She turned to watch them go, two grayed heads curved toward each other like magnets, their shoulders a little bent by the years, but happy. Their smiles had said so. The way they held hands said so.

She looked down at her empty hands, and tears welled up again.

No. It was over. Here she stood, right now, in this lovely town. She would find Lila and they would talk and she would find a job and make a new life and Kevin and his new girlfriend could just go fall off the earth for all she cared.

She could. She would. They should.

She strode down the promenade and imagined herself as someone who lived here, someone who belonged. She'd smile at everyone. She'd say hello and comment on what a beautiful day it was, for it really was, with the soft breeze off the water and the sunny skies. Even people who lived here noticed it, judging by the good-looking guy sitting in his car looking out the open window. She caught a whiff of what smelled like ripe, sun-warmed, sweet grapes and—coffee. Strong coffee. Good.

Following her nose, she found a quaint, brick-sided café with tables spilling out onto the sidewalk and the divine scent of fresh baking and espresso enough to drive a person hungry. Her stomach growled, but she really needed to watch her pennies. Full of regret, she passed the establishment by. She also passed a cute little clothing boutique, a kitchen and garden knickknack store, and a day spa before finding the address she'd been looking for. Not that she needed the address. She'd recognize the house anywhere, even after all the years that separated her from that long-ago summer.

Sure, the heritage-style two-story home might have been repainted a blazing white, but it still had its broad porch on three sides of the main floor and red trim around the windows. New plantings of brilliant red and white garden beds contained well established hedges and an emerald green expanse of lawn that hadn't been there before, but the same hanging copper planters around the porch held lush baskets of more red and white flowers. A new, neat red and white sandwich board sign set by the curb said: *This & That: Jewelry and Unsung Treasures* in a Celtic script. A discreet little sign in the window said "open."

It was the same house—at least she thought so. Except way back when there'd been no *This & That* sign and the place in her memory had been a little run down. Lila's grandparents had been old enough they'd had trouble keeping the place up. But that summer had been a wonderful time in her life and maybe, just maybe, she could reclaim it. Besides, she needed a safe place to pick up the pieces of herself and put herself back together into someone who didn't just go running after the first guy who said they liked her. Back then, Peachland and Lila had helped her when she'd been broken-hearted after her first boyfriend broke up with her.

Maybe Peachland and her old friend could help, now, too.

It was a sorry comment on her life that she was sort of counting on it.

CHAPTER 2

Brett Main spotted the woman while he was putting off dealing with the inevitable. He sat in his racing green Miata with the top up under a shade tree with the windows rolled down trying to get up the courage to face his sister. It was a long time coming, this meeting, and he wasn't looking forward to dealing with Chloe and her 'magic' stones and all her woo-woo, half-baked spiritual stuff, but he had to see her to deal with Mom and Dad's estate. He swallowed back the too-familiar lump of grief that choked his breath for a moment and looked out at the lake, clear as a good Riesling wine. The swimming beach would be packed with teenage girls showing off their shiny new bodies and moms would be riding heard on their youngsters like a vintner waiting for his wine's maturation. The lifeguards would have their hands full today.

It was better not to think of the loss of his folks and just focus on the business of the day—the science of living. Just like winemaking, each year's success was the result of last year's careful thought and planning of the use of his varietals and if this year didn't fully work, then next year's would take into account what had worked or not worked in the past. Treat this whole darn thing as one more logical step toward life and put his loss behind him. In this instance he needed Chloe's sign-off on the sale of their parents' house. His hypothesis was that the incentive of a little cash in her pocket might make that option attractive, regardless of the layers of memories stacked up in the old homestead along with too much furniture. Yes, that was the tack he was going to take.

He reached for his briefcase, but a shock of color went strolling by like a nicely chilled Chardonnay.

Well, perhaps not strolled—danced more like. She was small, petite, but the word "pixy" came to mind—from where, he wasn't sure given fairytale creatures weren't exactly his thing. Sunlight caught in her golden hair like a crown and she wore one of those loose, brightly colored sundresses that he usually abhorred for their shapelessness, but on this woman it didn't look shapeless at all. Nope. The breeze pressed it in softly in all the right places and the sunlight shone through just a little too brightly and showed the shadows of long slim legs through the fabric. Pretty. Very pretty from the back and practical, too, given the flat heels of her shoes and that the daypack she carried was pretty similar to the one he carried when he went out tramping the vineyard checking the vines. Definitely not anyone he knew from Peachland, so she had to be one of the summer people.

He watched her flutter down the street like a zing of pepper on the palate and wished she'd turn around. He'd step out of his car and maybe just happen to strike up a conversation, just like he'd done too many other times to count. A group of young women would stop by the vineyard's tasting room and be impressed that the assistant vintner took the time to explain the wines. Then he carefully selected the woman he liked best and asked her out for dinner. Just like that. He could do it with his eyes closed. But he'd sworn off summer people after Mom and Dad died. They'd longed to see him settle down. The trouble was, he never really was the settling down kind.

And the girl walking away down the promenade wasn't exactly his type, anyway. Too small, too blonde and likely too practical, too. Given the shoes. Yup, not his type at all. Definitely not the type who would swoon into his arms after one too many samples at the Elkhart Winery tasting room.

Focus, Main. Focus. You came here today with a specific purpose—now get it done and get back to your office. Besides, you swore of skirt-chasing, remember? Take a break after your parents' deaths?

He gave the woman in the bright floral dress one last look of regret. Climbing out of the car, he grabbed his briefcase that held all the research on area housing sales figures and realtor options. Faced with the information, there was only one logical course of action.

Of course when had his sister ever been logical?

§

Holding her breath, Kylee pushed open the door to *This & That* and a small bell chimed that reminded her of Asian temples. Coming up the stairs had been a challenge to her determination. Stepping inside? Well that was the test. It meant admitting defeat and asking for help. She hadn't done that since she was a kid, but everything else was gone now and she just needed a friend. That was all. Just Lila's friendship would give her the strength to start again.

The faint scent of incense and a sense of being watched met her like a cloud when she stepped inside. The former came from a burning incense stick uncoiling smoke from a spot near an ancient cash register. The latter came from a woman maybe a few years older than her who looking up expectantly from her spot behind the counter. Not Lila. Not Lila by a long shot, and Kylee almost turned on her heel and left.

But the shop was intriguing with its bevy of gleaming glass cases that filled its aubergine and gray-painted walls. It had old fashioned wire mannequins draped in Tibetan turquoise and coral necklaces she recognized from her time in India. Unique amber pieces as large as her thumb hung from copper hooks along one wall. Another wall was filled with a glass cupboard that seemed to hold a cornucopia of what looked like Mexican and Indian silver earrings as well as pieces from places she didn't know. The glass counters held what must be expensive, custom jewelry. In corners and in the window displays were peacock-shade scarves and what looked like finely crafted gloves and handbags. The richness of the decor shouldn't surprise her because Lila had always been a unique person of exquisite taste. It was a shop she'd love to spend time in, to explore and gather the many wonders from so many places in the world.

The woman behind the counter absently shifted her single long brown braid over her shoulder. She'd obviously been examining the books on the counter. She was of average height—still tall to Kylee, and wore a long flowy caftan thing and matching flowing trousers the color of clotted cream that only emphasized her slim figure. The three quarter sleeves exposed arms covered in silver and stone bracelets that matched the tangle of chains and stone pendants that hung around her neck. She had a pretty face and smooth skin and deep blue eyes that seemed to verge on lavender. Whatever she'd been waiting for, at the sight of Kylee, a look of surprise crossed her face. An inner tension seemed to drain away and the woman radiated a calm that Kylee could never imagine feeling.

Around the shop, pot lights spotlighted glass jewelry showcases to advantage and kept the store a comfortable cool despite the baking Okanagan day.

"May I help you?" The woman glided around the counter. She had bare feet with red toenails. She smiled and it was like being welcomed into a room with a fireplace and a cup of hot cocoa or something and that was strange. In all her travels, she'd never felt that welcome.

"Um. I'm just looking I guess." Escape out the door, or accept the welcome? Hadn't she been running long enough? She had to stop somewhere.

The woman cocked her head and her eyes narrowed a little. "Heart," she said.

Kylee froze. "Excuse me?"

The woman grinned and waved away Kylee's momentary tension. "Sorry. I do that. I meet someone and a word comes to mind. It usually is a true descriptor of the person. In your case I got two. Words that is. Heart and capable." She frowned and looked Kylee up and down. "That doesn't mean you have a capable heart because yours has some bruises on it."

Kylee would have laughed at that thought if the whole thing hadn't been so strange.

"Of course it might, given time. People often have to learn to assimilate their two halves into a whole." She flourished her arm around the shop. "I'm Chloe. Chloe Main. Welcome to *This & That*."

Chloe ran her hands down the long silver and stone necklaces she wore. Many of them were pale yellow.

She must have caught Kylee's glance because she held one of the stones up. "Chrysoberyl for calming. I'm expecting someone and not looking forward to it."

Which must be why she'd looked surprised when Kylee arrived, but the woman seemed okay, if a little strange. Like someone lost from the 1960s or '70s flower child age.

Kylee looked around, trying to end the conversation, or find the way to ask about Lila.

"Well, you feel free to browse. There's lots to see. Are you looking for anything in particular?" Chloe asked.

"Uh...." Come on Kylee spit it out would ya? "I—I was looking for Lila—Lila Weber—but I guess she doesn't live here anymore."

The woman—this Chloe—seemed to close right in on herself. She crossed her arms. Her chin came down, and even her beatific smile turned down slightly as if she suspected Kylee of some kind of crime.

"Fan of hers, are you?" Her voice was light, but it felt like a trap.

Kylee nodded. "We were friends in high school. I was hoping to reconnect."

"Really? What high school was that?" Chloe asked.

"Centennial Secondary. In Coquitlam and then Port Moody when they changed the school catchment boundaries." She glanced up at Chloe, but the woman's intense gaze made her uncomfortable. She looked away and noticed a display of unique sterling jewelry made of silver discs embellished with Sanskrit blessings and Buddhist symbols. She went over to it and hung over the glass display, her hands behind her back. "I haven't seen her in years, but one of my favorite memories is of coming up to Peachland one summer with her to stay with her grandparents. This was their house. I knew she'd moved here so I thought I'd pop in to see her." If Lila had sold the place and moved on, just what was she going to do? It hurt to think that she might have lost her friend for good.

She leaned more closely over the case. Such intricate work, it reminded her of snake scales or chain mail. It would feel cool and smooth against the skin. "These are really beautiful."

Chloe straightened and she instantly dropped her Earth-Mother persona to become a sales person. "You've got good taste. Those are custom-made pieces by Regulus, a local designer. They've been popular enough that they've even shown up on New York catwalks.

Interesting. To some people it might even be impressive. But when you're broke it really didn't mean anything at all.

"I love those earrings with the small disc and the temple bell." Her hand went to the simple gold hoops in her earlobes. "I'll bet they're expensive, though."

"Let's check, shall we?" Chloe grabbed her set of keys, the necklaces rattling around her neck as she unlocked the cabinet. She pulled out the earrings for Kylee to examine. She felt the woman's study like a hot brand on her skin—probably picking up on her dress's signs of wear and the old daypack on her shoulder—not exactly the kind of customer who could afford one-of-a-kind jewelry. But she had to hand it to Chloe. She was polite.

Kylee held the earrings up to her ear and peered into the hand mirror Chloe steadied for her. They'd show off her neck and jaw line. Kylee flipped over the discreet price tag, shook her head sadly, and handed the earrings back.

"Too rich for my blood, I'm afraid. I've just come back from six months of travelling." She stuck out her hand. "I'm Kylee Jensen."

Chloe didn't hesitate to accept her hand yet it seemed to make her thoughtful. Then she brightened. Her hand was warm. "Pleased to meet you. I really am. Like I said, I'm Chloe. Lila isn't here right now, but she'll be back later. I'm one of her partners."

It was like Kylee had passed a test or something, because suddenly Chloe's suspicion disappeared. The woman still studied her as if she could categorize her like she did her stones. Chrysoberyl for calming, indeed. Get real, please. But Chloe's gaze seemed like a sponge that took in everything from the slight fraying around the neck of Kylee's dress, to the state of her well-chewed fingernails.

The door bell chimed behind them and Chloe seemed to stiffen.

"Hey, Chloe."

The deep masculine voice turned Kylee around.

Unlike most men, this one didn't look foreign to a shop so purpose-built for women. He stepped farther into the room and a faint scent of sunshine and warm grapes heady as wine reached her. Him.

Tall, she thought. Good looking, just like she'd thought when she'd spotted him sitting in his car. Brown hair in a thick rumpled thatch that kept falling into his eyes like a kid. He shoved it impatiently back over his forehead as his gaze skittered from Chloe to Kylee and back, as if he couldn't decide who to focus on. That sent an instant flush up her shoulders.

He had high cheekbones and a narrow, refined nose that led down to a full mouth that was a lot like Chloe's. Same shade of hair, too. A brother? Related, certainly. But though Chloe's eyes were deep blue that seemed to change color almost to violet as she moved around the room, this man's eyes were a pale green like the first poplar leaves in spring. He wore tan khakis and a rich brown polo shirt that set off his eyes very nicely, thank you very much.

"Uh, hi," he said and nodded in Kylee's direction. His gaze lingered a moment too long so she had to look away. Then he stepped up to Chloe. "I need to talk to you." But his gaze snuck back to Kylee for a moment.

Chloe seemed to stiffen and all the warm shop-keeper persona disappeared into that suspicion Kylee had seen earlier. This time it was directed at the intruder. All the air seemed to have been sucked out of the room and Kylee's chest closed up. There was conflict here.

She didn't do conflict anymore—not if she could help it.

So hard to breathe. So hard to move. Just like all the times Kevin had yelled at her. Even if this guy wasn't yelling, even if he was Chloe's relative, he was no one the woman wanted to see at the moment, that was clear from the way Chloe folded her arms over her chest and retreated behind the counter. Kylee so didn't want to get caught in the middle of someone else's family drama. She'd had enough drama of her own for a lifetime. The shop that had seemed so friendly and intriguing with all its unique displays suddenly seemed too cluttered, crowded, dark. She really needed to get out of here—back to the sunshine and wait somewhere else until Lila returned.

Brett and Chloe's attention was on each other so she edged toward the door. Just a few more feet and she could be out of here.

"Kylee? Where are you going? You don't have to go. Brett here, is just leaving."

Two sets of too intense eyes turned toward her and her voice escaped her. But Brett didn't really look like he was going anywhere any time soon.

She shook her head mutely, pushed out the door and ran.

The wooden stairs thumped under the rush of her footsteps. At the sidewalk she looked left-right-left, uncertain where to turn. Her car was that way. Maybe just get in the car and drive again? To somewhere else? The trouble was, coming to see Lila had seemed like her last stand. She'd been running so long that she really had nowhere else to go.

Head down, she hurried toward her car, threading blindly past the summer-clad people blissfully walking their dogs or jogging together down the promenade. Everyone was with someone. The sunlight placed too-bright dancing motes on the rippled water. The willows swayed long limbs to catch her. No. That was being silly. She stopped and leaned her hands on her knees and just inhaled. Moisture and heat and coconut suntan lotion that just took her away to that happy summer so long ago. She'd loved Peachland then and she thought she could love it now, except for that Brett guy. He was too pushy, too forceful and focused on himself and she'd had enough of guys like that. She took a deep breath, straightened and marched down the sidewalk following the scent of the coffee shop, and stepped inside. No way was she going to let Brett whatever his name was, chase her away from Peachland.

When she left it would be her decision.

Maybe.

To read more of *Unlocking Her Heart*, look for it in your favorite bookstore or on-line retailer, or find it at
www.karenlabrahamson.com

Romance, Fantasy and Mystery

from Twisted Root Publishing

If you enjoyed this book, you might
enjoy other titles available from
Twisted Root Publishing in your local
bookstore or wherever e-books are
sold.

www.twistedrootpublishing.com

www.ingramcontent.com/pod-product-compliance
Lightning Source LLC
Chambersburg PA
CBHW050352190726
48284CB00007BB/2248